THE SABAOTH'S ARROW

BOOK 2 OF THE BAKA DJINN CHRONICLES

J F MEHENTEE

1

Roshan had already folded her arms when she noticed her foot tapping.

'We have to hurry,' she called to the daeva in the other room. 'Guardsmen have entered the city. We have to leave —now.'

'Daniyel, get out from under there,' the woman said. 'This isn't a game.'

Roshan stalked across the small living area towards the bedroom. A fire burned in the hearth; the woman had been kneading a ball of dough when Roshan had arrived.

Inside the bedroom, the woman lay face down on the floor and was reaching under a bed. Roshan heard giggling.

'Got you,' the woman said. She pulled.

A child, only two years old, appeared from under the edge of the bed. The woman stood and hauled her son into her arms.

'Here,' the woman said, and thrust the child at Roshan. 'Hold him while I pack some things.'

Roshan took the child before his mother could drop him. Daniyel, the front of his tunic covered in dust from under the bed, eyed Roshan with suspicion.

'I told, you,' Roshan said, impatience sharpening the edge to her voice, 'there are guardsmen in Arshak.'

The woman had found a bag and now searched for items to pack.

'We don't have time for this,' Roshan said.

Daniyel wriggled in Roshan's arms.

'I'm going, and I'm taking your child with me.'

Roshan headed for the door. She stomped, hoping the woman had gotten the message. Daniyel waved his hands and shook his head. She'd made it a third of the way across the living area when the woman spoke.

'Shouldn't we wait for my husband?'

Roshan tightened her hold on Daniyel. He'd started to slip through her arms.

'Your husband sent me. He's with my brother and the other daevas. I'm the only one who can raise a portal. The others are waiting—we have to go.'

Daniyel's lower lip trembled, and a tear collected in the corner of an eye. To Roshan's relief, the woman took the boy from her.

Roshan led the way, the woman close behind.

The daevas of Arshak lived in the south-eastern quarter of the city. There was no paving but sand, and some buildings were made from salvaged wood rather than stone. Roshan doubted Arshak's administrators visited this part of the city often. The daevas avoided the streets and moved around by using the dark, tight alleyways between the ramshackle constructions.

'Where are we going?' the woman said.

The high magus and his army weren't due to reach Arshak until tomorrow morning. Roshan and Navid were supposed to be here to inform the daevas about Sassan's imminent arrival, not evacuate them to Baka. With news that dispatches from the high magus and his general were now being destroyed instead of being archived in Persepae, anticipating the empire's next move had become a challenge.

'We're going to the disused stable,' Roshan said. She turned and saw that the woman had stopped. Daniyel clung to his mother's neck, a dent between his downy eyebrows.

'There's a quicker way,' the woman said.

Roshan followed. If she had a better idea of the stable's location, the quicker and easier solution would be to raise a portal. There hadn't been time for her and Navid to conduct a survey of this neighbourhood, let alone the city.

As they ran, Daniyel's head bobbed, though his eyes never left Roshan. Worried he might cry and draw attention to them, Roshan pulled a face.

Dimples appeared in Daniyel's cheeks. He rested his chin on his mother's shoulder and continued staring at Roshan.

Daniyel beamed with delight when Roshan nearly collided with his mother. Roshan took her lead and backed into the alleyway.

'Soldiers,' the woman whispered.

Daniyel crossed his eyes and stuck out his tongue.

Four guardsmen, armed with spears, patrolled the street they had to cross.

If only I knew where the stable was.

'Is there some way we can go around them?' Roshan said.

The woman thought for a moment.

'Play,' Daniyel said.

Roshan pulled a face.

Daniyel didn't look impressed.

The woman shook her head.

'We'd have to go back the way we came.'

At this rate, they'd end up running in circles and leave Navid stranded with the other daevas. There had to be another way.

'Play,' Daniyel demanded.

'Shush, dear,' the woman said.

Roshan slapped her forehead.

Daniyel mimicked her.

'I'm sorry, I should have asked this earlier,' she said. 'Can you give me the coordinates for the stable?'

The woman's eyes narrowed.

'You said before that you could raise a portal. But you're not djinn.'

She didn't have time to explain.

'Please, the coordinates, and I'll show you.'

The woman squinted as she translated the stable's location into portal coordinates. Roshan wove a destination window and then peered through it. The stable, one of its double doors missing and part of its roof fallen in, sat on the opposite side of a street. She saw a face peering out of the shadows next to it.

'What's Navid doing over there? He should be in the stable.'

A guardsman walked past the destination window, making both Roshan and the mother jump. Daniyel nodded and giggled.

'Again,' he said.

Roshan adjusted the window's coordinates with a quick incantation. The image shifted from the stable to some thirty steps behind the alleyway Navid hid in. The alleyway was so narrow, the light from above only partially lit the ground. Roshan could just make out the alleyway's dead end. She adjusted the incantation to reverse the window's direction. Daevas filled two-thirds of the cramped alleyway. Another adjustment and the window looked on to the alleyway's opening and Navid. Roshan raised a boarding window and fused it to the destination window.

'Hah,' Daniyel said, his forefinger tracing the azure circle of Roshan's portal.

'You first,' Roshan said, smiling at the woman's surprise.

The lines on her brother's face softened when he saw her emerge from her portal.

'What took you so long?' he said, more intrigued than annoyed.

4

She nodded at Daniyel.

'Someone wanted to play at hiding.'

Daniyel beamed, then clapped his hands.

'I like hiding,' he said.

Roshan and Navid put their fingers to their lips. Daniyel did the same, then bounced up and down in his mother's arms.

Navid jabbed his thumb at the alleyway's entrance.

'We can't enter the stable without being seen,' he said. 'One of us wandering inside there might not draw any attention.' He glanced behind him. 'But there are over fifty daevas back there.'

Roshan wracked her brain for somewhere else in the city they might go. Life as a novice and two years spent with Yesfir had honed her memory, and she only had to repeat a piece of information once to remember it. But she couldn't recollect anywhere else on the crude map Shephatiah had sketched for them where they wouldn't be seen.

'There's some space at the end of this alleyway,' Roshan said. 'It's dark, and so long as we take our time and don't do anything to draw attention to ourselves, we could enter Baka from there.'

Lines reappeared on Navid's face.

'Another alley opens on to this one.' He pointed behind him. 'Halfway down. That's how we ended up in here. We'll need someone to keep an eye on both entrances.'

Roshan glanced behind her.

'You stay here. I'll raise a portal and then cover the other one.'

A corner of Navid's mouth crimped. He nodded.

'All right,' he said. 'Right now, it's the best we can do.'

Daniyel and his mother had already disappeared into the crush of daevas. The woman had to be searching for her husband. As Roshan squeezed her way through, she saw how the daevas preferred to huddle close together instead of moving farther down into the alleyway.

Roshan passed the woman, who'd found her husband.

Daniyel, squashed between his parents, grinned and then stuck out his tongue.

She reached the far end of the alleyway. With little room to manoeuvre and having to shoulder her way through so many, Roshan found herself breathless and sweating. She wasted no time in raising a portal to Baka. The azure of her portal caught the attention of those in front of her.

'This way,' she said, keeping her voice low.

In the portal's light, she saw heads farther down from her turn in her direction. A murmur filled the alleyway. Roshan hoped the sound didn't carry to either of its entrances.

She pressed her back to the wall and sidled past the daevas who approached the portal. They moved at a steady rate, but not as fast as they could have if the alleyway were wider.

Roshan heard crying coming from the alleyway's centre. She'd spotted other children on her way to the far end of the alleyway. It might not be Daniyel.

The crying turned into a wail.

Shut the child up.

She felt her bracelet pulse and knew Navid was thinking the same thing. Roshan shook her head. She should have erected a dome of invisibility and silence around them before raising the portal. Now it was too late. She began the incantation for a dome of protection.

'Soldiers,' someone yelled from the front.

'We'll hold them off,' another shouted. 'The rest of you at the back, get a move on.'

An elbow dug into Roshan's side, and a passing shoulder shoved her hard against the wall, driving the air from her lungs and leaving her with no breath for the rest of the incantation. In the corner of her vision she saw those daevas at the back of the alleyway rushing through the portal. The press from the front, however, caused some daevas to lose their balance. Roshan's feet scuffed against the ground, and her back scraped against the wall.

Her nails clawed at the brickwork as the crush of daevas dragged her closer to the portal.

Opposite her, the abandoned stable's wooden wall gave a loud creak. Roshan saw it warp against the weight of the daevas. The wall screeched before the wood split and collapsed inwards. Daevas disappeared into the hole.

Roshan dropped to the ground and landed awkwardly on her ankle. Thankfully, no one pressed against her ribcage, and she could breathe again.

Roshan's ankle buckled under her own weight, and she dropped to the ground. Someone's shin struck her cheek, the force of the impact smashing the back of her head against the wall. Golden light exploded behind her eyes. She tasted blood. Roshan held a protective hand in front of her face and tried to push herself back up with the other. All around her, daevas stumbled, held on to each other and tried to regain their balance.

A foot kicked her hand from under her, and she landed on her side. A hand, not her own, pressed down on her exposed side as the daeva above her tried to right herself.

Roshan felt her side give and knew one or more ribs had cracked. She screwed her eyes shut. Fearful of being crushed, she cried, 'Stop!'

Feet scuffed the ground. Thuds filled the alleyway and air escaped mouths in hisses. Snaps and tears swiftly followed.

Roshan didn't have to open her eyes to realise she'd made a terrible mistake.

2

E mad's mood hadn't lifted as he returned to the deep sweep of tents ahead of him. Baka was sand-filled, dilapidated, uninhabitable and defenceless. Right now, the daevas' new home comprised nothing more than a camp.

What were you thinking, Fiqitush? What have you seen that I and everyone else is blind to? What's so special about this ruin you're insisting the daevas make their home?

Two days had passed since his rescue in Derbicca. Yesterday, he'd offered to visit Baka as an excuse to get away from his brother. Emad loved him dearly, but Fiqitush was almost as zealous about Baka as the high magus was about the One Religion.

Emad strolled past the first line of tents and spied a group of daevas leading others from a portal. He'd seen several of these groups at work during the past two hours. Their job was to receive those daevas whose city lay in the path of the high magus and his army. Each member of the semicircle would show a displaced daeva their tent, list the rules and mealtimes and recite Fiqitush's unrealistic promise: Baka would soon be free of segregation—thanks to daeva madness being cured—and become home to daevas and djinn alike.

Something different about this group, however, caught his attention. Four daevas leaned forward as they watched whatever was going on behind the destination window the djinni, who kept his distance, had woven for them. A daeva placed an arm across the shoulders of his neighbour, who shook his head.

Emad hurried over to them.

The djinni's destination window hovered over a network of alleyways that opened on to a street. In one particular alleyway—a daeva pointed at it for Emad—lay what he took for bodies. They lay both inside the alleyway and just beyond what looked like a hole in the side of a building. Emad saw a handful of soldiers enter the building. He took a step closer when one of the bodies in the alleyway moved.

'Deepen your window's focus, please,' he said to the djinni. Emad leaned in for a closer look. 'Are those daevas I'm looking at?' he said, to no one in particular.

The djinni nodded.

Emad couldn't believe what he saw.

'Those are daevas down there.' He pointed at the destination window. 'And they're moving. Why aren't you helping them?'

He looked around at the other daevas and recognised fear.

What have we become?

Emad straightened and glared at the djinni.

'I want a scimitar and I want you to raise a portal to the inside of that building now.' The djinni hesitated. 'You know who I am.' He gazed at the other daevas. 'I'll hold off the guardsmen. I want you to get as many of those daevas out of there as you can.' One of the daevas took a backwards step. 'Those are our brothers and sisters. They need our help.'

'There's another djinni in the camp, Your Highness,' the djinni said. 'She and I will help you.'

Emad nodded.

'Good man,' he said.

Armed with the scimitar the djinni had woven for him, Emad stepped through the portal.

Three soldiers pulled the struggling daevas through the hole in the wall. Two more forced them to line up at spearpoint. Iron in the spearheads sucked at Emad's energy. It reminded him of being manacled in Derbicca. The memory inflamed him. Back then, he'd missed the opportunity to kill the high magus, which was why the persecution of daevas like these continued.

Emad waited a few moments for two other daevas to emerge from the portal, both carrying scimitars.

He charged in the same moment the two soldiers holding the daevas at bay spotted him. He waved his scimitar and then shouldered into the first soldier.

Emad landed on top of him, but not before they'd collided with his comrade. With the first soldier wriggling beneath him, Emad rammed the tip of his scimitar into the thigh of the fallen soldier in front of him. The soldier cried out, his hands no longer gripping his spear but his upper thigh. Before the soldier beneath him could push him off, Emad rose and thumped him with his scimitar's pommel. He only dazed the soldier and had to hit him a second time.

Emad looked around. One of the daevas who'd arrived from Baka sat on the ground, a small pool of blood soaking into the earth and straw around him. A female djinni gestured with her hands as the three other guardsmen clutched their necks, their faces red and their eyes bulging.

Emad got to his feet, ran past the suffocating soldiers, acknowledged the djinni and then entered the hole in the wall.

Daevas, some standing and others struggling to, filled the dark, narrow alleyway. Across from him he recognised a young woman, more a girl, really. She had accompanied Yesfir to Derbicca and had led Administrator Arman to his doorstep. Emad had trouble believing Fiqitush when his brother had told him how this same girl had saved Behrouz's life by channelling her auric energy into him and, though temporarily, turning him and Yesfir back into djinn.

What's she doing here?

The girl stood. Grazes covered one side of her face, and a sleeve had been torn from her tunic's shoulder. Perhaps because of the poor light, her face looked as if it had turned a dark turquoise colour.

The girl limped farther into the alleyway and then raised a portal. Silently, she ushered people towards it. She looked shaken. If he hadn't noticed her trying to look past those approaching the portal and its azure light, Emad would have gone over to her. He stood on tiptoes and craned his neck. The djinni who'd woven the destination window in Baka stood at the alleyway's entrance. Two soldiers jabbed at the entranceway with spears, their spearheads distorting and blurring the air.

'A dome of protection,' Emad muttered. 'Good man.'

He leaned his scimitar against the wall and stepped into the middle of the alleyway, hoping to restore some order. Like the girl —Roshan, he remembered her name now—many of the daevas had scrapes and cuts. Some nursed a forearm or a hand. One man leaned on a woman for support. Beyond that pair, one-third of the alleyway remained filled with daevas who hadn't yet gotten up.

What happened here?

Emad slid past the injured and knelt before the first daeva he came across. He found a pulse, then patted her cheeks to wake her. She didn't respond, so he shook her shoulders gently. Still she didn't wake.

He looked up and wondered if the other fallen were in the same condition. Emad stepped over the woman and knelt in front of a male daeva. The pupils of his open eyes remained dilated. Emad found no pulse.

Further ahead, Emad saw a groggy-looking young man

picking his way among the fallen. He stopped, bent down and then squeezed his eyes shut.

'Navid?'

The young man looked up and past Emad.

Roshan sidled along the alleyway's wall to reach the young man she'd called out to. Emad could see they were siblings. If not for Fiqitush, he'd never have known they were twins.

With light from above and the entrance, Roshan's skin looked normal, flesh-coloured.

When Roshan reached her brother, she looked down. Navid caught her before her legs gave way. Roshan clamped a hand to her mouth, but not before a wail of despair escaped it.

Emad threaded his way among the fallen. He stopped when he saw the child, a boy of two years. The side of his head touched his shoulder. The child's neck was broken.

'Prince Emad.'

Emad looked over at the djinni who'd raised the protective dome. With his hands held out, he continued to renew the dome's integrity as soldiers on the other side jabbed at it with spears and hacked at it with short swords.

'They have iron weapons. I'm getting tired. I won't be able to renew this dome for much longer.'

Emad nodded to the djinni.

'You two,' he said, addressing the twins. 'We have to go.' He saw recognition dawn on Roshan's face. He shook his head before she could say anything. 'There's no time to help them. We have to go—now!'

The word snapped Navid out of his daze. He took his teary sister by the elbow. Satisfied the pair were doing as they were told, he stepped over and between the fallen to reach the hole in the wall.

Like the djinni at the front of the alleyway, the female djinni had used a protective dome to prevent more soldiers from entering.

'We're going,' he called to her.

She acknowledged him with a nod.

Emad stopped himself from turning left. He went right and back to the unconscious woman.

You can't save them all, he told himself.

Emad slid his arms under the daeva. While he couldn't run more than two hundred paces without having to catch his breath, his strength hadn't deserted him. Emad hauled himself up and covered the now-clear alleyway. Those capable of leaving were in Baka.

He waited beside the portal.

The twins approached, Roshan carrying a different child to the one she'd discovered, and Navid, impressively, carrying a daeva draped across each shoulder.

Back in Iram, Emad had rolled his eyes as Fiqitush extolled the twins' virtues. Just now, he'd glimpsed something of what made them special.

But that didn't mean he'd let Fiqitush off so lightly. He'd have questions for his brother, and after what he'd just seen, he had better have some good answers.

3

Armaiti never tired of the vista, the way the sunlight reflected off the three snowy mountain peaks. The view calmed her, helped her think.

Her plan, the one she'd made after Emad's rescue in Derbicca, might work against her. Through a dream and disguised as a lamassu, she had shown Roshan how to channel her auric energy to the daevas. Roshan had only done so for Behrouz and Yesfir, but she now had a means of channelling energy to all the daevas. In time, and disguised as her nemesis, Manah, she'd show Roshan how to do just that. She'd even tell Roshan it would weaken her. Knowing the girl's inclination for helping others, and after what had just happened in Arshak, Roshan would willingly agree. And Armaiti had more in mind for Roshan, but now she had to provide Sassan with the means of countering Roshan's rekindling of the djinn's and daevas' auric energy.

Armaiti materialised as an eagle-headed spirit. She folded her wings, bent down and began to scoop away snow with her taloned fingers. She felt a prickling beneath her feathers and saw a lamassu, Manah, staring at her, a disdainful look on his bearded human face. Armaiti ignored him and continued to dig. Her former adversary and now a construct of her imagination— one she'd made to highlight the rightness or wrongness of an intended action—did not move his bull's body to stop her or flap his wings in anger. His silence and lack of action felt like a condemnation.

'The Unmade Creator told me to bury it here after Solomon died,' she said, hating herself for justifying her actions. She glanced up at the sky, then continued with her digging. 'If It didn't want me to use the seal, It would have told me to destroy it.'

Manah neither moved nor spoke.

Tangible as heat, heat that didn't melt snow and ice, the seal's power touched her fingertips. The signet ring, with a hexagram composed of two interlaced triangles, lay inside permafrost, which Armaiti melted with a thought.

The brass ring grasped firmly in her fist, Armaiti looked over at the lamassu and found Manah had gone.

What does that mean? she wondered.

She could drop the ring back into the hole, cover it over and let Roshan do whatever it was the Unmade Creator wanted her to do.

The ring thrummed with the accumulated power of the djinn nation in her balled hand.

Or was this what the Unmade Creator expected of her? Had It set her up to be the cause that produced the effect It expected to see in Roshan?

'I want Roshan dead,' she said to the sky. 'And I think You want me to kill her. Why else, instead of destroying it, would You have told me to bury the seal? If You don't want me to do this, tell me, show me—do something.'

She berated herself for justifying her actions as those mirroring the Unmade Creator's intentions. And Armaiti hated herself for still hoping the Unmade Creator's silence was all part of Its plan, that once she'd reached her goal and rid this world of

Roshan, It would release her and allow her access to her domain.

The seal's power throbbed against her palm. Except for the sound of the buffeting wind, she received no reply.

'If You didn't want me to do this, You would have stopped me days ago,' she said.

Armaiti launched herself into the air and flew towards Arshak.

4

Emad found his brother seated at a table in his chambers. Fiqitush put down the tablet he'd been reading.

'From the look on your face, I'm guessing you weren't impressed by Baka.'

Emad bunched his brow.

'Have you heard what happened in Arshak?' He didn't wait for an answer. 'Adults and children have been injured or killed trying to escape Sassan's soldiers. Those twins of yours bungled the evacuation by raising a portal in a narrow alleyway. They made it impossible for anyone to make a fast escape. It's obvious they're inexperienced, Fiqitush. Why did you put them in charge?'

His brother rested his elbows on the table and rubbed his face. He looked tired. Nineteen years had passed since they'd last met. His brother looked as if he'd aged by a century.

'Compared to the last time you were here, there are more daevas than djinn.' Fiqitush's chest fell with a sigh. 'You're right about Roshan and Navid, but there's no one else to spare who can weave magic and raise portals. Things are desperate and likely to get worse now that Sassan and his army have changed direction and are heading east. It's as if he knows about Baka.'

Fiqitush was right. Thanks to his obstinance and using Aeshma as an excuse not to meet his brother, what had happened in Derbicca now stretched the djinn and put the daevas in further danger.

'I've been here two days, Fiqitush. You haven't yet told me what you want and why I'm so important to you.'

Fiqitush rose from his chair and gestured at the cushions scattered in front of a clothes chest.

'Sit down,' he said, then waited until Emad sat cross-legged.

'You sit down too,' Emad said. 'I'm not getting a crick in the neck looking up at you.'

Seated next to him, Fiqitush said, 'When I built Iram, used the auric energy I took from the seal, I didn't realise I'd bound myself to it.'

The resignation behind Fiqitush's words troubled Emad.

'You're not making sense,' he said. 'What do you mean, you bound yourself to it?'

His brother ran a hand over his head. Emad recognised his brother's nervous tic.

'Did you think I sent all those messengers because I am king, because it's beneath me to visit my brother?'

Status had never motivated Fiqitush. If he'd wanted to visit him in Derbicca or at sea on *Apkallu*, he would have. Fiqitush had always made it clear kinship came before kingship.

Emad gazed about the sparse room. Columns of tablets either side of the table gathered dust, and a broken stylus lay beneath it. A rolled-up rug leaned against a corner. Since his last visit, his brother had really let the place go. No, that wasn't right.

'The magic holding Iram is failing because...' Emad couldn't bring himself to say the rest.

Fiqitush nodded, his eyes downcast.

'My auric energy is fading. Our people have been generous

and donated the remains of their auric energy to help preserve my vitality. There were five hundred of us when we settled here. Now there are barely a hundred.' He shook his head. 'I had hoped retrieving Solomon's seal might have changed all that, severed the bond between me and this place. Iram fell into disrepair over the decades I spent searching for the seal. On my return, I couldn't reverse the decay. I knew then I could never leave Iram again.'

Emad held his breath for a moment. Fiqitush's auric energy was fading. No wonder his brother had kept sending djinn. Fiqitush stared at him as if to say, *Save your apology and regrets for another time.* Emad swallowed. His brother was neither demonstrative nor sentimental.

'Why have you stopped searching for the seal?' he said, hoping there was some way for Fiqitush to dodge his situation. 'There's still time. This place has started to crumble, but it isn't exactly falling apart.'

To Emad's annoyance, Fiqitush smiled their father's patient and sympathetic smile.

'Thanks to Roshan, it doesn't matter.'

Roshan, again!

'I just got back from Arshak, remember. Even if she's special, she's still inexperienced.'

Fiqitush nodded.

'You're right. She and her brother still have much to learn. They will need someone to support them. Roshan has tremendous potential to do good, *if* the right person is around to mentor her. With Roshan supporting us, there's no need to go after the seal—for now. There'll be time later on for you to recover it.'

Again, Emad heard the familiar connotations as Fiqitush spoke. His brother knew something that had escaped him.

'Why do I get the impression you're talking about me when you talk about Roshan? If anyone should mentor her, it's you. You were the one trained to rule while I rowed on the river.' He waved a hand to prevent Fiqitush from interrupting. 'You could get her to restore your auric energy, like she did Behrouz and Yesfir.'

Fiqitush wouldn't meet his gaze.

'I won't deny the thought hasn't crossed my mind. I'd like to feel the sun on my face again and do so without the weight of a city dragging me beneath the surface.'

Emad sat up. It was if Fiqitush had unbolted a door through which Emad could escape.

'Then ask her to do it. Regain your vitality, Iram's vitality, and then mentor Roshan.'

Fiqitush laughed.

'What's so funny?'

Fiqitush's eyes widened and the ends of his lips rose.

'You, you're funny. Do you remember the word you used with Father when you said you wanted nothing to do with rulership, didn't want the responsibility?'

Emad rolled his eyes.

'Of course I don't. That conversation happened centuries ago.'

Fiqitush leaned in.

'I remember. The word you used was *categorical*. I admit it was a big word for you, little brother, but you meant it. Just weeks after my coronation, you bought a ship, hired a crew, explored the world and had adventures. You led those men, and they followed you everywhere. I kept an eye on you, Emad. Over three hundred years, you captained thirty crews of two hundred humans. That's six thousand, all together. More than I've reigned over in the same time. Not bad for a djinni who avoided responsibility. And then, nineteen years ago, you turn up here with a magus. She needed your help, and you protected her.' Fiqitush clicked his fingers. 'What was her name?'

Emad glared at his brother.

'You know her name. It was Shafira. You can stop now. You've made your point.'

Fiqitush shook his head.

'Have I? After centuries of sailing the world, leading and mentoring the men and women who crewed your ships, you gave it all up, without complaint, to care for Aeshma.' Fiqitush leaned back and pointed. 'You, brother, are the most responsible person I know.'

Emad felt cornered and outmanoeuvred. He might have countered with what had happened to Aeshma, but he wasn't about to bring up their cousin's death for the sake of an argument.

'All right,' he said. 'So, I can be responsible, but I still don't see what this has to do with Roshan needing mentoring and why it should be me.'

His brother's joviality vanished, making Emad's stomach twist.

'Because, while you sailed the world, experienced it, I spent all of my time down here. Everything I know about the world is through the eyes of the other djinn.' He shook his head. 'What could I possibly teach Roshan and Navid? Besides, it's time the djinn returned to the surface instead of hiding away underground. They need a leader who knows the world, can show it to them and show them how to be safe.'

It was Emad's turn to laugh.

'You speak as if the djinn are children, Fiqitush. You make it sound as if they've regressed under your reign.'

Fiqitush nodded, his lips thin and white.

'How can you agree?' Emad said. 'Iram, everything that's brought us here, is Solomon's fault and God's fault. It's not your fault the djinn went into hiding.'

Fiqitush reached over and patted Emad's arm.

'Calm down, brother. I'm just telling you how things are. It doesn't matter whose fault it is. What matters now are the djinn's and the daevas' futures. The djinn have lived in hiding too long, and the daevas are a shadow of the djinn they once were. That must change, and they'll need a leader, not a ruler, to make it happen. For now, their fate rests in Roshan's hands, and Roshan will need a worldly mentor, an advisor who will be patient with her and tolerant of her mistakes.'

His brother had given the subject a lot of thought. But one thing made little sense.

'Though I don't like it, I understand what you've said about the djinn and daevas. If Roshan were ever to come for advice, if it were within my sphere of knowledge, I'd give it—just like I'd give it to any djinni or daeva who asked. On the other hand, I don't see why I have to be her mentor. I don't see why you've singled *me* out when patience and tolerance aren't my best qualities.'

Fiqitush nodded.

'I won't disagree with you about that. But with the right incentive, you'd develop your patience and tolerance until they were your best qualities.'

Fiqitush had the annoying habit of discussing a matter without getting to the point. It was a sign of nervousness, a way of putting off news or information he thought was unpleasant.

'I know you're trying to tell me something, let me down gently. Just get to the—'

The realisation struck like a kick to the chest. Emad had to stop himself from rolling backwards and falling off his cushion.

His brother had feigned forgetting Shafira's name. He'd pretended to remind Emad of her.

Emad had brought her to Iram to keep her safe. He'd comforted her, and she'd done the same. According to his brother, that was nineteen years ago.

He looked up and saw Fiqitush nodding.

'That's right, Emad. Shafira conceived the twins here in Iram. Navid and Roshan are your son and daughter.'

5

Roshan tapped the firestone's surface several times. Its pale red glow changed and filled her room with golden light. The brightness failed to banish her despondence and the image of the child: the side of Daniyel's head too easily touching a shoulder, his eyes open and unblinking.

Whatever the motivation behind Armaiti's *destroyer* dream, the sabaoth was right.

What good was weaving sabaoth magic if it did more harm than good? She had tried wishing away the magic, and when that had failed, she'd attempted to banish it with spoken words. It had remained, a part of her she couldn't understand or control.

She heard the rattle of glasses on a silver tray and then a knock on the door.

'Can I come in?'

For the first time since their return from Arshak, the surrounding gloom withdrew a little.

'Come in,' she told her brother.

He'd brought mint tea, which he set on the floor in front of her bed. Roshan got up and perched herself on its edge.

'How are you feeling?' he said, pouring hot water into the glasses filled with mint leaves.

'I can't stop thinking about all the daevas we left behind.' Roshan paused, waiting for the image of Daniyel's broken neck to disappear. 'I want to go back and rescue them all.'

Navid sat and wrapped an arm around her. Roshan nestled against his shoulder.

'I know how you feel. It's no one's fault. The djinn are spread too thinly. Things would have turned out differently if those guardsmen hadn't arrived early—don't you think?'

She nodded, although it did nothing to dispel the recurring image of a lifeless Daniyel.

'What good is sabaoth magic if I always end up hurting people?'

Navid gave her a comforting squeeze.

'Innocents always get caught between opposing sides,' he said. 'But that mustn't stop us from taking a side and doing what we believe to be right.'

She lifted her head from his shoulder and gazed at him.

'Since when did you become so wise?'

Navid grinned and his cheeks dimpled.

'Actually, I heard Yesfir saying it to Behrouz.' He bent down, picked up both glasses by their rims and offered her one. 'We're all worried about what this sabaoth magic is doing to you. Yesfir said you have to make a choice about whether to continue using it. She thinks not making a choice will only make you unhappier.'

Roshan sipped her tea. Yesfir was right, but making a choice wasn't that easy. Remorse at what had happened in Arshak gnawed at her.

'Well,' Navid said, and put down his glass, 'I'm hungry again. The shape-shifting I've been practising is playing havoc with my appetite. You missed lunch. Come with me—you need to eat.'

Food was the furthest thing from her mind, and she told him so.

'You go,' she said. 'I'll rest a little longer.' She raised her arm. Her tunic's cuff fell to reveal the silver bracelet. 'I'll come find you with this,' she added, then gave the bracelet a tap. 'I'm getting better at using it to communicate with others.'

She continued to sip her tea after Navid had left. It gave her something to do with her hands. The mint's aroma helped her to forget the stench of the alleyway: the sweat, the fear and the blood.

Drinking tea, however, didn't stop the tears, tears she couldn't decide were for her or Daniyel and all those she'd left behind in Arshak.

Her glass empty, Roshan bent down to refill it. She stopped when she saw a hoof next to the silver tray. She saw a second adjacent hoof and behind them another pair. The smell of clean straw, burning cedar wood and myrrh filled her nostrils. The glass slipped from her hand and shattered when she looked up and saw a bearded human face looking down at her.

Roshan had seen pairs of the protective spirits guarding palace and temple entrances. Those lamassu were made of stone. This one had a taupe hide, real feathers in its wings, and ringlets of hair for a beard. Just like the ones she'd seen on guard, this lamassu was so large, the cap covering its head scraped the ceiling.

The lamassu shrank until its head was level with hers.

'I'm sorry,' it said. 'I never meant to frighten you.'

Compared to his stern countenance, his voice sounded gentle. Roshan wiped the tears from her cheeks.

'Your tears are for the daevas, Roshan. There's no shame in shedding them.'

Surprise overtook her fear.

'You know my name?'

'Of course,' the lamassu said. 'I've known you since the moment Armaiti saved you. Like her, I wanted to see the human-djinn child. I told God what she did. It punished her for interfering with one of Its creations.'

Once, to have seen such a thing, a living lamassu, would have astounded her. She just wanted to be alone and for protective spirits and sabaoth to leave her be.

'Why are you here?' she said. What she wanted to say was *Are you here to punish me?*

'I'm here to help you.' The lamassu tilted his head at her. 'I can show you what it takes to control sabaoth magic.'

The lamassu's sudden appearance didn't feel right. There was no telling whether she was taking to a protective spirit, a sabaoth or something entirely different.

'If you've known me as long as Armaiti has, why have you chosen to appear now? If you're here to help, why didn't you before Armaiti pushed me off a roof in Derbicca?'

Thanks to his long beard, Roshan found it difficult to read the expression on the lamassu's face. His dark brown eyes narrowed ever so slightly, and his forehead creased.

'Because I had to wait until God, who we call the Unmade Creator, gave me permission,' he said. 'I often take this lamassu form for humans. It makes it easy for them to understand who and what I am. Like Armaiti, I'm a sabaoth. God's rules bind the sabaoth, one of which is never to interfere with Its creations. Only when It has a task for us are we allowed to become visible and to communicate with you. God is unhappy with what Armaiti has done, and so It has sent me to help you.'

Roshan had begun to believe God had abandoned this world and left it to the whims of His sabaoth. She looked the lamassu in the eye.

'Instead of helping me, why don't you just get rid of Armaiti?'

The lamassu shifted its weight, as if ready to take a backwards step.

'If that is what God wants, then It would order me to *get rid* of Armaiti. It has Its plans, plans too complex for the likes of you and me to understand. What It wants is for you to understand sabaoth magic as deeply as you understand human and djinn magic.'

Roshan remembered Yesfir's words about her happiness and not making a choice. God sending this lamassu didn't make the choice easier. After what had happened this morning, she just wanted to be left alone and allowed to go back to the way things were a week earlier. What would happen if she took the lamassu up on its offer, an offer endorsed by God? Was it possible she'd be unhappier than right now?

'If I accept your help, what do I have to do?'

'Come with me. Leave Iram so I can train you without distractions.'

The doubt niggling at her intensified. She shook her head.

'No. I'm not leaving here. Do you honestly expect me to do such a thing?'

The lamassu nodded, his smile one of amusement.

'You're right. You need time to consider my offer, *and* I need to prove you can trust me.' The lamassu's eyebrows rose. 'Am I right?'

'Yes,' she said, returning his nod.

'Very good,' the lamassu said. 'I have two pieces of information to prove my trustworthiness. The first is a question I suspect you already know the answer to.' The lamassu took a step forward. 'Who do you think sent you the desert dream—the dream in which you shared your auric energy with the daevas?'

Roshan gripped the edge of her bed to stop herself from covering her mouth. She saw no sign of pride or amusement on the lamassu's face.

'The other piece of information takes the form of a warning.' He stepped closer until only a handspan separated them.

'You may have helped restore auric energy to two daevas, but that won't be enough. The djinn and daevas are in dreadful danger. Armaiti plans on using Solomon's seal against them. You will have to choose between returning to a human way of life or battling Armaiti and the seal. If you fight, human and djinn magic won't be enough against her.'

As he backed away, the lamassu's hooves clattered against the stone floor. His body widened, his legs lengthened and his wings unfolded.

'My name is Manah,' the lamassu said. 'When you are ready to receive my help, call out my name.' He faded. 'Until then, farewell.'

Roshan stood, her legs shaking and her heart pounding at the news Armaiti had the seal.

'Wait,' she said, the lamassu a pale outline. 'Come back—come back, Manah.'

Although the scent of myrrh lingered, Manah had gone.

What did Armaiti hope to do with Solomon's seal? Why was she so set on hurting the djinn and daevas?

If you fight, human and djinn magic won't be enough against her.

It took several deep breaths to calm herself. She opened the door to her room and stopped. He'd spent years searching for the seal. The news would devastate the king. Roshan shook away the thought. He had to know. If the djinn and daevas were to resist the seal's power and fight back, the sooner the better.

6

Zana sat beside Father. Above them, the sun had passed its zenith. With two hours to wait before the next portal's appearance and the latest arrivals to be welcomed and assigned to their tents, Father had found a shaded and secluded spot inside Baka for a nap. Mother had told Zana to keep an eye on him. Roshan might have healed his wound, but he still needed to rest.

Father slept under the shadow of the ziggurat. The desert winds had sandblasted its walls smooth, and a wide crack ran up two-thirds of it. It didn't look the safest of structures to take up residence in, and according to Father, no one had gone inside to check if it contained anything more than sand. The wall Father leaned on had fared little better, the sand heaped against it on the other side propping it up.

Zana listened to Father's breathing deepen. Arms folded across his chest, legs stretched out and also crossed at the ankles, Father's head drooped forward.

Since they'd arrived there, Father had confirmed the rumour of a manticore den existing somewhere up in the mountains. The manticores moved among the daevas and djinn as humans, providing help wherever needed. Zana, however, hadn't summoned the courage yet to ask permission to go look for the den. To Zana, searching for his own kind was like turning his back on his foster parents.

To his left, close to the west watchtower, half of which lay hidden beneath sand, Zana spied a girl climbing the slope of sand leading to the battlements. She had a bag slung over her shoulder and wore a robe instead of leggings and tunic.

There was no one else up on the battlements clearing away sand, and if the girl were leaving the city, the battlements were an unusual route to take. Zana wondered. Baka's north and south walls faced mountains. The ocean lay eastward, and the desert lay westward. Was there a route up into the northernmost mountain from the battlements? Was this how the manticores entered and exited Baka?

Zana stood. He hesitated, unsure whether to wake Father and tell him where he was going. Mother did say he needed his rest. Before he changed his mind, Zana bounded towards the hill of sand. He ran with his head up, his eyes fixed on the girl halfway up the mound. By the time he reached the bottom, the girl had disappeared over the parapet.

Zana scrambled over the sand, splaying his paws to prevent them from sinking too far. He reached the top panting, his face dripping with sweat. There was plenty of space for him to squeeze between the crenellations. Sure enough, on the other side of the battlements was more sand heaped against them. Below him, the girl neared the bottom.

Zana took several deep, calming breaths. The girl had to be a manticore. If she'd just turn around, then he could recognise her the next time he saw her inside the city.

'Wait,' he called. The girl continued her descent. He called out again. She didn't stop or turn.

Behind him and down below, Father leaned against the wall and slept.

'Sorry, Father,' he said under his breath, and then jumped over the parapet.

He dug his hind legs into the sand to slow himself and to prevent himself from sliding. The girl had reached the bottom when Zana called out to her again—better to let her know he was behind her than for her to discover she was being followed.

The girl shrugged off her robe, and Zana's voice caught in his throat. The sight of her bare back made him lose his footing. He slid down the slope on his belly. He glided over the sand too quickly for his paws to gain any grip.

The slope levelled, and he slowed. A shadow passed in front of him. Only, it wasn't a shadow, because Zana collided with it and bit his tongue. Before he could back away, something hard struck his side and pinned him to the ground.

A male face, three times the size of a human's or djinni's, glared down at him. He had skin as dark as ebony, and his amber eyes seemed fathomless.

'You are trespassing,' the giant head said, and then growled. 'This territory belongs to the Cross Scar pride.'

Zana swallowed. Black, wavy hair framed the face—a mane. Above him loomed a male manticore, a huge manticore. Claws dug into Zana's side as he struggled to rise. The best thing to do, if he wanted to avoid being shredded, was to lie still.

'I just wanted to say hello,' he said.

The manticore's amber eyes continued to bore into Zana. He didn't know if he'd pacified him or made things worse.

'Vul,' a female voice said.

The voice came from behind Zana. With Vul's paw pressing down on him, he couldn't twist his neck far enough to see who it belonged to.

'Get off him. You're hurting him.'

Vul pressed a little harder before raising his paw. Zana rolled onto his feet, stood and backed away until his tail touched the slope of sand behind him.

'Why didn't you just say hello instead of following me?'

A female manticore stared at him. She had the same amber eyes as Vul, although her skin was the colour of blanched almonds. From her size, he guessed she was his age. The bag she'd slung over one shoulder now hung from her neck.

'When I saw you climbing up to the battlements, I thought you might be a manticore,' he said. 'I wasn't sure, so I followed you.' He glanced at Vul. 'I called out, but you didn't hear me. I didn't know this was your...territory.'

The female manticore padded towards him. Unlike Vul, she smiled.

'My name is Nahrian,' she said. 'And you've met my brother, Vul.'

Vul raised his chin at the mention of his name.

'Hello, Vul. Hello, Nahrian.'

Vul's eyelids drooped.

'You've said your *hello*,' Vul said. 'Go back to where you came from. And leave my sister alone.'

'Vul!' Nahrian said. She stomped over to her brother and snarled at him. 'You don't decide who I make friends with.' Like Zana, she was only a third of Vul's size. The male manticore stepped sideways to put some distance between him and his sister.

Nahrian smiled apologetically when she faced Zana. Zana found himself confused by her sweet smile and her indifference to her brother's size and fierceness.

'There's no need to introduce yourself, Zana,' she said. 'We've heard the daevas talking about you and how you protected Roshan in Derbicca. Your pride must be proud of you.'

The compliment stung.

'I have a foster mother and a foster father, but I don't belong to a pride.'

Nahrian dropped her gaze.

'Oh, I never meant to—'

Zana shook his head.

'Oh, no, you mustn't feel bad. A circus stole me from my pride. Yesfir and Behrouz found me and gave me a home, and they became my parents, my pride.'

Vul snorted.

'*Stolen* from your pride. Is that what you think happened?'

Zana's hackles straightened.

'Of course I do. How would you know?'

Vul shot Zana a contemptuous stare.

'Because I *see* things, past and future.'

Zana glanced at Nahrian. Had Vul spoken the truth? Could he do that?

Nahrian nodded, her brow bunched.

He looked back at Vul and didn't avoid his stare.

'What have you seen, Vul?'

The male manticore smirked.

'I've seen that you can't keep your promises.' Vul lowered his head a fraction. His eyes turned to slits. 'And I know you want to shape-shift. Get used to the way you are, Zana. You lack the self-discipline to learn and practise that skill.'

The conviction behind Vul's words intimidated Zana more than the manticore's size. Was it true he couldn't keep promises and lacked self-discipline?

'Not everything Vul sees comes true,' Nahrian said.

A growl rumbled in Vul's chest. However, he didn't contradict his sister.

'Is that true?' he said to Vul. He stopped himself from flinching when the manticore lifted a paw.

Vul's smile made Zana shiver.

'The future changes. So, like my sister says, some things don't happen the way I first see them. But I've seen enough about you, Zana, to know that you'll fail even the simplest test we set our cubs.' He raised his head and gazed southwards. Vul pointed with a paw.

Zana followed his gaze.

'I'm confident you won't last an afternoon up there on that ledge without water and without moving.'

Zana's first thought involved getting permission from Mother and Father. He squinted. There'd be no escape from the sun on that exposed rock shelf. It would be torture to sit up there without moving and to go without water for half a day.

Nahrian took a step forward, then smiled reassuringly.

'I completed the test,' she said. 'I'm sure you could too.'

Her encouragement made him blush. Had he looked so scared?

'Well?' Vul said. 'Will you accept, or will you decline and prove that, besides lacking discipline, you're a coward?'

He was no coward, and Zana sorely wanted to prove the frightening and arrogant Vul wrong. Zana raised his head and looked the male manticore in the eye.

'I accept,' he said. 'I'll take your test.'

7

Roshan heard muffled voices behind the door to the king's chamber. A while back, she'd crossed her legs and sat down. Whoever was in there, the exchange sounded heated. From all the rising inflections, a lot of questions were being asked.

To avoid eavesdropping, she replayed her conversation with Manah, the lamassu. After this morning's events in Arshak, it wasn't fair she should be the bearer of more bad news.

For the umpteenth time, Roshan sifted over what had happened in Arshak.

Should I accept Manah's offer? she wondered.

'Roshan, what are you doing down there? How long have you been waiting?'

Prince Emad stood in the doorway, his eyes fixed on her as if he'd seen a malevolent spirit. Behind him, the king peered over the prince's shoulder.

'How long have you been waiting?' the king repeated.

Roshan pushed herself up and shook her head.

'I don't know—an hour, maybe.'

The prince blanched.

'I was, um, visited by a lamassu, another sabaoth, and it had a message.'

'Another sabaoth?' the prince said. 'Are you all right? Did it hurt you?'

The king shoved past the prince and shook his head at his brother.

'The corridor isn't the best place to talk,' he said. 'Come inside.' He waved her in.

Apart from a rolled-up rug, a table and chair, a bed and a clothes chest—a tunic's sleeve poking out and beyond the lid—the king's chamber was sparse. Her nose wrinkled at the dampness pervading the room.

The king sat down on a cushion and gestured for both the prince and Roshan to join him.

'Next time you want to see me, don't stand on ceremony; just knock on the door,' the king said. 'Now, what's this about a lamassu?'

Roshan described her meeting with the sabaoth named Manah and how he'd appeared to her as a lamassu. While she spoke, the prince stared at her so intensely, it made her uncomfortable. When she reached the part about Armaiti retrieving the seal, the king wiped his bald head with a shaky hand. He kept swallowing as if he were about to choke.

The prince wrung his hands and shook his head.

The king pursed his lips, then opened them with a *smack*.

'Solomon named the sabaoth who gave him the seal as Armaiti. She's had it all along.' He screwed his eyes shut and curled his hands into fists, making his forearms shake. When he opened them, he gazed at Roshan with stony eyes. 'Did this other sabaoth, Manah, say what Armaiti planned on doing with the seal?'

Roshan shook her head.

The king stared at her. Unable to hold his gaze, she glanced at the prince, who looked down as if he'd done something wrong.

What's his problem?

'You, Roshan, you siding with us, has gotten Armaiti worried,' the king said. 'I think that's why she'll use the seal against us.'

The prince's head snapped up.

'Roshan and Navid have to leave Iram. They're both in danger, and they're putting Iram in danger. I could arrange for them to board a ship, sail off somewhere.'

Roshan intervened.

'Armaiti knows how to find me,' she said. 'I know I speak for Navid, too, when I say I want to stay and help. It's better for everyone if I confront her instead of running.'

The prince snorted.

'How's it better for everyone if you stay here and put them in danger?'

Before she could answer, the king reached across and touched his brother's knee.

'Because Manah showed Roshan how to restore a daeva's auric energy. Whatever it is Armaiti has planned for us, we're powerless unless Roshan stays. Manah's offered to help her understand the sabaoth magic. She and that magic are all that stand between us and Armaiti annihilating the djinn and daevas.'

Roshan reminded herself the king was talking about her and not a mythical warrior who battled sabaoth. To hear him talking like that dried her mouth.

The chamber was silent, and it looked to Roshan as if an unspoken argument passed between the brothers. Whatever it was, it didn't matter. Roshan wouldn't let them decide for her or Navid.

'Navid should be here before we decide,' she told them, ending the silent stalemate. 'Let me get him. I won't take long.'

The prince opened his mouth to reply. King Fiqitush placed a restraining hand on his shoulder.

'We understand,' the king said. 'Find Navid. We'll wait for you here.'

Roshan thanked the king. She walked to the door, fighting the urge to run. There was no decision to make, she had to remain and help, but the prince's insistence that she leave Iram made her doubt herself. His arrest and Aeshma's death were her fault. No wonder he considered her a danger to herself and others.

After turning Navid back into a human, the king had assigned him the room next to hers. She strode to it.

The room was empty.

Roshan touched her bracelet, closed her eyes. Using her mind, she constructed an image of his room and then whispered, 'Navid.' She opened her eyes when the bracelet pulsed. He'd heard her call.

Roshan wanted to collapse onto Navid's bed. No, she'd use the time while waiting to consult Manah and find out how he could help her. She closed her eyes and called out his name.

The scent of myrrh and a giant lamassu filled the room. Roshan sat up. Manah shrank until his eyes were level with hers.

Before she could tell him why she'd summoned him, he spoke.

'Armaiti has the seal,' he said. A destination window appeared to his left. 'Look for yourself.'

She recognised the snow-capped mountain range with its three prominent peaks. Just beyond the lower edge of the window was a hole, a heap of snow next to it. The destination window zoomed in on the hole. Roshan wasn't sure what Manah wanted her to look at.

'It's a hole,' she said. 'So?'

The edge of the window flickered. Manah had woven a boarding window and formed a portal.

'Put your hand in the hole and tell me what you feel.'

Roshan imagined Manah collapsing the portal while she rooted around inside it.

Manah frowned.

'How disappointing,' he said. 'Remember, God wants me to

help you, not harm you.'

He'd made her feel foolish. She got off the bed and squatted in front of the circle of violet light. She inserted her hand through the portal and then down inside the hole.

The freezing air made her skin pimple and numbed her fingertips. Even though she'd lost her sense of touch, the power emanating from the hole was palpable. It tugged at her arm so hard, she had to lean back and place most of her weight on her back foot.

'That's a scrap of the seal's power,' Manah said. 'Armaiti's activated its magic.'

With most of her weight on her back foot, Roshan drew her arm from out of the portal.

'What's Armaiti going to do with the seal?' she said. If what she'd felt was only a trace of its power, what kind of harm was it capable of?

'She'll use it to destroy the djinn and daevas, of course.'

Manah had said it so matter-of-factly and as if she were a simpleton for asking.

'What could she possibly have against them? What have they done to deserve such hate?'

Manah's forehead creased, and one corner of his mouth lifted.

'Because she's trapped on this world, and the only way to escape it is to destroy it. But only a few of her sabaoth powers remain. She's no longer omnipresent and she can't create or destroy matter. She needs the humans to do that for her. The djinn and daevas are the only race who can stop them. That's why she wants to be rid of them.' Manah squinted at her. 'And then there's you. When Armaiti saved you, her sabaoth energy lay dormant within your aura. Then, when you were gravely injured in Persepae, it healed you. Now, each time you're injured, more of the energy is activated. Your aura is one-third human, one-third sabaoth and one-third djinn. If you're hurt again, sabaoth energy will supplant either your human energy or djinn energy. You'll grow stronger and become more of a threat to Armaiti. That's why you must regenerate the djinn's and daevas' auric energy and fight alongside them.'

Roshan sat back on the bed and held her head in her hands. Images of the alleyway in Arshak filled her mind.

'Me fighting—you make it sound so simple.'

Manah's hooves tapped against the room's stone floor.

She looked up from her hands and met Manah's self-satisfied gaze.

Manah raised his chin, his face imperious.

'Come with me.' The portal opening out onto the snow-covered mountaintop flickered. The destination window had changed to dawn rising over an arid canyon. 'Come with me now, and begin your training, Roshan.'

If it meant she could fight and be confident she'd hurt only Armaiti, she had to go. As soon as she'd mastered the magic, she'd return to Iram.

Roshan stood.

Navid.

She couldn't leave without telling him where she'd gone. He didn't have a tablet for her to leave him a message on, and she didn't want him and the others to worry.

Roshan touched her bracelet. There was no way of knowing how close or how far he was.

'Roshan,' Manah said. 'It's time to go.'

With her fingers still pressed against the bracelet, she stared at the wall behind Manah.

'I have to go. I'm going to learn about sabaoth magic. Please don't worry. I'll come back soon.'

The walls hissed and cracked with the words she'd burned onto its surface. If he didn't receive or understand the message she'd sent via the bracelet, he would after he entered his room.

Roshan turned her attention from the wall to the lamassu.

'I'm ready, Manah. Let's go.'

8

E   mad studied his brother's face as Fiqitush gazed at the
    bare wall in front of him. Fiqitush looked as if his spirit
    had excused itself from the room.

'What do you think Armaiti will do with the seal?' Emad said.

Fiqitush continued to stare, although he squinted now.

Emad listened as his brother explained Roshan's encounter
with Armaiti in Derbicca. He wanted to interrupt him, remind
Fiqitush how Roshan had arrived outside his home soon after
her encounter with the sabaoth, but stopped himself. His brother
often recounted information before he answered a question.

'Armaiti told Roshan she's stuck on this world. As punishment
for saving Roshan, God limited Armaiti's powers. For example,
unlike the sabaoth as we understand them, Armaiti can only be
in one place at a time. Perhaps there are other things she can't do
without the seal's help.'

Emad rubbed his chin.

'It's a strong possibility,' Emad said. 'But what if she repeats
what she did last time and gives the seal to a human and gets
them to do her dirty work?'

Fiqitush screwed his eyes shut and then rubbed them with thumb and forefinger.

'The golden arrow she gave the high magus killed Aeshma and almost killed Behrouz. If she gives Sassan the seal, we're finished.'

Emad wanted to cover his face with his hands and shake his head.

'With or without the seal, our lives would be easier if Sassan weren't around,' Emad said.

Fiqitush stopped rubbing his eyes.

'What do you mean?'

'In Derbicca, you tried to kill him while rescuing me. We should try again but this time take a more subtle approach.'

Fiqitush frowned.

'We're talking about the high magus. There's nothing *subtle* about killing the empire's religious leader.'

He waved a calming hand at Fiqitush.

'I won't say any more. It's best I keep the details to myself—in case we have an unwelcome guest. Someone must keep a close eye on the high magus to see if he receives the seal.'

His brother regarded the ceiling as though Armaiti hovered above them.

'And what if the high magus doesn't receive it?' Fiqitush said.

Emad shrugged.

'Does it matter? The high magus holds over thirty daevas prisoner. He'll use them to set an example to the others. Soon, there won't be any daevas left to become djinn again.' He sat up as he warmed to the subject. 'With Sassan out of the way, there'll be more time to move the remaining daevas to Baka. With the extra time and daevas, you'll be able to speed up Baka's restoration.'

Fiqitush pondered Emad's words with his faraway stare. Eventually, he nodded.

'I could have done with your help sooner, Emad. But I'm glad, finally, you're here.' Fiqitush reached over and rubbed Emad's shoulder. 'All my plans have failed, brother. By now, the seal should be in my hands and Baka restored using djinn magic. Having you here, having Roshan and Navid here, gives me hope.'

Emad thought of Aeshma. He bowed his head.

'I'm sorry I took so long. I've been selfish and a fool.'

9

Manah's portal opened on to the most unusual river basin Roshan had ever seen. Columns of rock looked as if they'd sprouted from the sandy ground and had grown as tall as trees. The rocks formed layers of red, orange and white on top of one another. The strangest thing was how the position of each colour corresponded with those of the adjacent pillars.

In the distance, beyond this forest of stone columns she spied conifers, a river and an orange-red sunset behind them.

'Where are we?' Roshan said.

Manah strode past her.

'So far away, nightfall approaches while it's mid-afternoon in Iram. Armaiti rarely watches this place.'

The lamassu strode past her and towards a narrow path leading down into the basin. When he didn't look back, Roshan hurried after him.

'The energy Armaiti used to save you has an affinity for your dual human-djinn nature, making it easy for it to bind to your aura.'

So, this is happening to me because I have djinn and human parents, Roshan thought.

Armaiti had saved her, and in doing so, she'd changed her in ways that were only becoming clear now.

The valley below had an eerie quality and made Roshan uneasy. Exactly how far away were they, and even if she had the coordinates, how much Core power would she need to return herself to Iram?

Stop thinking, she told herself. *Just listen to Manah and see where he's taking you.*

'Back when Armaiti saved you,' Manah continued, 'the energy she'd used bound itself to your aura. It remained dormant until a few days ago, when you were fatally injured in the chancery. The injury reawakened the same energy that had saved you as an infant, and then it saved you again. Armaiti knew this might happen, but God's punishment prevented her from altering your aura a second time.'

Roshan had thought Yesfir had saved her by sacrificing her auric energy. If, according to Manah, Armaiti's auric energy had saved her, had the djinni's sacrifice been for nothing?

'The sabaoth auric energy is also changing you, Roshan. The more you weave sabaoth magic, the more it alters your body.'

Manah spoke at a speed that made it impossible for Roshan to interrupt him. She made a note to ask him what she was changing into and why—twice, her skin had turned blue-grey.

'Unlike Core power that humans and djinn summon from the earth, the sabaoth summon energy from their Domain—the boundless space in which this world resides. A sabaoth's domain is vast and contains one billion trillion stars and thousands of worlds like this one. That is a lot of power to call upon. And because it is free of the physical laws governing this world, incantations, symbols and rituals have no effect over it. Domain power is different from Core power because it isn't just raw power to be summoned and shaped to serve your needs. Domain power is *alive*. It anticipates all possible desires, and it *knows* how to realise them. That's why it's woven with thought, which is essentially what a sabaoth is, *pure thought*.'

Roshan listened. She understood the words Manah used. The concepts they described were a different matter: power that was alive and anticipated your desires, and the sabaoth being pure thought. The words were repeatable, memorisable even, but she couldn't explain them.

'Remember, God has punished Armaiti by removing most of her sabaoth powers. If you're to beat her, you must work on how you think. Your thoughts must be perfectly clear to yourself and to the Domain power you summon.'

They'd reached the basin, and Manah stopped between two of the towering, striated rock pillars.

'Come here whenever you need to practise magic,' Manah said. He raised a hoof and tapped it twice against the ground. A breeze out of nowhere blew away the sand and scree that had slid down the valley slopes.

Roshan took a step back and recognised the symbols left behind.

'Coordinates,' she said. Just like Manah's words, she recognised the positions they described but not where in the world the destination window opened on to. 'Are they for here?'

Manah nodded.

'Now you've seen this place, you can either think yourself a portal or use those coordinates to raise one. You'll need more Core power to raise a portal, but the sabaoth energy your aura contains will heal the scarring.'

He said nothing about how much it would hurt if she used djinn magic to raise a portal. Composed of nothing but thought, Roshan guessed pain wasn't Manah's concern.

'Here's the first of two exercises I want you to practise.'

In place of the coordinates, pieces of charcoal covered the ground.

'Choose a lump, Roshan, and point at it for me.'

She pointed at a piece the size of her fist and halfway between the centre of the pile and her feet.

'Thank you. Now watch the lump closely.'

Roshan bent forward, her hands resting on her thighs. The corners of her eyes tightened.

'One. Two. Three,' Manah said, a pause between each count. 'Pick it up, please, and put it in front of my hoof.'

Warm to the touch, the charcoal whiffed of tar. Roshan stepped back. Manah stamped on the lump with his hoof.

The lamassu retreated from the broken pieces of charcoal. 'Please, take a look.'

Most of the pieces were black. Here and there, she found an edge coated in white, powdery ash. Roshan was about to ask what she was looking for when she saw a rough, opaque stone the size of her little finger's nail. She held it up for Manah to see.

'Diamonds grow under tremendous pressure. I placed the centre of the lump under the pressure a mountain might exert if it were on top of it.'

Roshan was confused. Manah had smashed the lump into smaller pieces to reveal the diamond. A mountain would have reduced the piece of charcoal to powder, or something else. Wouldn't it?

'Your turn, Roshan. You have a go.'

Roshan's palms turned sticky. She examined the uncut diamond and then dropped it into her pocket. Using djinn magic and an alchemic incantation, she could produce a diamond from anything, including charcoal. She knew there was a point to this exercise, but she didn't know what. She pointed at a piece of charcoal on her right.

'That one.'

'Good,' Manah said. 'Now imagine the charcoal under a lot of pressure, and the pressure increases. Just that piece, mind.'

Roshan closed her eyes and tried to conjure the image of a

mountain, its triangular tip pressing down on the charcoal she'd chosen. She imagined the mountain's weight increasing through its centre and an opaque crystal forming beneath its tip.

'Ready,' Manah said. 'One. Two—'

Something touched her mind, as if a gentle breeze had entered her head.

'Three.'

Roshan smelled burning and opened her eyes.

Before her, the entire pile of charcoal was aflame.

Manah's eyes never left the fire.

'Before you applied pressure, did you experience anything?' he said.

It was hard to tell if Manah expected all the charcoal to catch light, or if he wanted her to learn something else from this exercise.

'A kind of coolness in my head. It's not something I'd feel while weaving djinn or human magic. Does it have something to do with that?' She pointed at the fire.

Manah shot her an approving smile.

'It does. That coolness—it's different for each sabaoth—is the Domain power warning you it wasn't sure what you wanted. What you got was the closest approximation of your request.'

She'd imagined making a diamond using pressure, just like Manah had told her. So, why the fire?

'Increasing pressure produces heat,' Manah said. He must have read her mind. 'The pressure you placed the charcoal under also created heat, which spread to the other lumps. Domain power tried to warn you this would happen. Next time you have a similar feeling, what will you do?'

Roshan was a novice again, back at the temple and sitting in a lesson. She'd never liked getting a tutor's question wrong, facing their ire and then the other novices' jibes.

'Well, Roshan, what will you do next time?'

While teaching her djinn magic, Yesfir had taught Roshan a

technique for calming her mind. Through controlling her breath, she could reduce her stream of thoughts to a trickle. It allowed her to focus her attention on the incantation.

'I don't know,' she said. 'I want to say *Stop the thought*. Even if I could control my thinking all the time, I didn't know that increasing pressure creates heat until you told me. How am I supposed to avoid making a mistake when I don't know why I'm making it?'

Manah smirked.

'Because you can't and because I tricked you. Remember, Domain power is *alive*, so let it think for you. Your thoughts must focus only on outcomes.'

Roshan chewed her lower lip. Manah had set her up to illustrate a point, but she didn't understand what it was.

'Focus on outcomes. What does that mean?'

Manah looked from her to the burning charcoal and back again. He snorted and shook his head.

'When you think about what you want, don't include the *how*; concentrate only on the *what*. I asked you to make a diamond. But I complicated things by telling you how to make it. Domain power knows how to make a diamond. You just have to tell it the size you want and if it's cut or uncut. Leave the rest up to Domain power.'

What Manah said made sense. It explained what had happened in Derbicca with Administrator Arman and his guards. In Arshak, when she'd told the scrum of daevas to stop, she hadn't thought how to make them stop, but neither had she been specific: *stop and stand still*. If Domain power had tried to warn her, she wouldn't have understood what she'd felt.

The pile of burning charcoals disappeared. In its place lay a trench, fifteen paces long and embedded in the basin's floor. Water then filled the trough. It bubbled, steam rising from its surface.

'As you discover the nature of Domain power and how to

49

shape your thoughts to weave sabaoth magic, you must learn how to weave magic as your situation changes.' Manah pointed at the trough with his chin. 'The water, as you can see, is boiling. In this exercise, you can't change the temperature of *all* the water in the channel, just the water surrounding the fish.'

A fish the size of Roshan's hand, its scales and fins pale pink, appeared above the trough and landed in the water with a splash. Roshan gasped. Through the steam and bubbles, she saw the fish swim the length of the trough, turn and swim back. Roshan stepped closer. The steam wet her face, and the heat rose the closer she got.

The fish stopped swimming directly beneath Roshan. Its fins undulated as it maintained its position among the rising bubbles. Its mouth opened and closed, and its gills flapped in time.

The fish, water and the trough disappeared so quickly, Roshan found herself staring at bare, flat rock.

'I want you to create ten diamonds, without setting light to the adjacent lumps of charcoal,' Manah said. 'You decide the size and cut. When you've mastered making inanimate objects, I want you to make a fish, a live one, and then protect it as it swims up and down a channel of boiling water.'

I'll cook the poor fish.

As a novice, she'd conjured plants and fruits, but never a living creature.

'What happens if I kill the fish?'

Manah raised his eyebrows and gazed at her despairingly.

'Then resurrect it and start again.'

With the right incantations, a necromancer could use human magic to resurrect an animal, although the results were unpredictable and often dangerous. Necromancers were former magi who'd abandoned the Divine Light and used their skills and magic for their own ends. What Manah wanted her to do, the high temple deemed unholy and shunned.

Manah must have read her mind again.

'You are not a magus, Roshan, and people have died because you wove sabaoth magic. If you want to stop Armaiti and save the djinn and daevas, you can no longer think like a novice or a magus. Your ability to summon Domain power makes you very dangerous. Whether or not you want to, you could destroy the world with a single thought. Consider that, Roshan, and then decide if resurrecting a fish is abhorrent.'

Manah turned and walked up the path they'd taken to reach the basin. Roshan dashed over and stood in front of him.

'You're not leaving?' she said. 'Aren't you going to stay and help me with the exercises?'

Manah tilted his head. The corners of his eyes creased and pulled his lips into a tight smile.

'I've given you much to think about and a lot to do. You must practise, sharpen your thoughts and make them pliant enough to anticipate all possible futures. If you have to, return to Iram, but I'd recommend you concentrate on the exercises without distractions. I'll come back this evening, and we'll continue your lessons.'

Manah sidestepped Roshan and continued up the mountain. She wheeled to watch him leave, unsure if she could achieve a fraction of what he expected of her by the time he returned. A half-dozen steps up the path, the lamassu faded and then disappeared.

10

_____

Sassan finished his morning prayers and opened his eyes. Light seeped through the canvas. It relaxed him to continue kneeling and watch how the flames in the fire altar consumed the cedar wood. The headache he'd woken up with this morning, however, hadn't eased.

Sassan stood. The amphora still lay next to the golden arrow. There hadn't been time to return the diluted poppy juice to the apothecary. He shook his head and left for the operations tent.

Outside, under a clear sky, the camp was already busy with preparations for the executions. He saw handcarts being drawn towards Arshak, their contents the platform he'd later stand on.

As expected, General Afacan waited for him inside the tent. The general stood.

'Think, speak and act well, High Magus,' he said.

'Think, speak and act well, General,' Sassan replied. He didn't wait to sit down before saying, 'What are the latest numbers for yesterday's trouble?'

Sassan sat down and the general followed.

'We captured thirty-five daevas. Seven are children. And there were two casualties—one a daeva child. Three djinn helped the daevas escape through a portal. One of them was the young woman in Derbicca who killed an archer with a scream.'

Sassan's insides quivered. He'd heard about the djinni with the scream and wondered if there were other djinn as powerful. Could he count on the sabaoth's arrow to stop djinn like her? He'd memorised the incantation the eagle-headed spirit had taught him. He could make more golden arrows.

Wait, he said to himself, *there's a better way to deal with this.*

'General, I want all thirty-five daevas executed. The executions will take place outside the city. We've a rebellion on our hands. I don't trust any daeva to keep their word after they convert. After what happened in Derbicca, they'll go on practising their magic, knowing that if they're caught, the djinn will come rescue them.'

The general didn't move. He looked as if he hadn't understood what Sassan had said.

'General?'

'The vast majority of daevas in Arshak have their own businesses. There was no need for them to resort to magic to earn a living. This sounds like we're executing daevas for being daevas.'

Sassan shook his head. At times, the general could be too soft on them. They had to quash the rebellion before it drew the emperor's attention.

'If they weren't practising magic, why did they run, try to escape down that alley?' Sassan said.

The general nodded.

'I'm still making enquiries about that. However, if we execute every daeva we arrest, we'll give them a reason to run.'

Sassan rubbed his temples. His headache had worsened.

'The evacuation of daevas from cities began weeks ago, General. When we arrive outside a city, the daevas we encounter are either too stupid to leave, too slow or want us to execute them before the daeva madness claims them. I've been a fool to believe the daevas would comply and embrace the One Religion.' Sassan curled his hand into a fist. 'I won't let them treat us like fools anymore. We must find Baka as soon as possible and exterminate the daevas and the djinn.'

The general cleared his throat.

'If all daevas are fleeing to Baka, why don't we just annex the city? They'd be easier to control.'

Why was the general being so soft on them and protecting them? Why couldn't he see this was God's work?

'The emperor has approved my request to take Baka,' Sassan said. 'I want you to request the reinforcements you deem necessary to reduce that city and its occupants to rubble.' He stood, and the general followed. 'Don't forget what happened in Derbicca, General Afacan. What happened yesterday is the first sign the daevas no longer respect either the emperor's authority or God's. Write the request and dispatch it today. Am I understood?'

The general saluted.

'Perfectly, High Magus.'

'Think, speak and act well, General,' Sassan said, and exited the tent before the general could reply.

Back in his own tent, it felt as if burning needles had punctured his head. Sassan hurried to the table, his hand hovering over the amphora.

The fire in the altar still burned.

Sassan knelt before it, clasped his hands together and prayed to distract himself. He prayed the emperor would grant General Afacan's request for reinforcements. Then he asked God for proof the djinn and daevas were a threat to the One Religion and deserved annihilation.

Instead of a worded answer, Sassan heard a *clank*. He opened his eyes. Something had landed among the blackened wood and grey ashes, and it had struck the metal tray beneath. Sassan retrieved his fire-tongs and used them to brush away the ash and wood.

If not for Baka's location on the wooden plaque and the golden arrow, Sassan might have felt wonder at the sight of the metal object sitting among the flames. In its place he experienced satisfaction and a deepening of his conviction. God wanted Sassan to succeed.

Sassan held up the object with the tongs and blew on it. It was a ring, a signet ring made from what looked like brass. It bore a hexagram for its seal. He recognised it not from tablets and papyri but from his days as a novice and his history lessons. God had instructed a sabaoth to make the ring and present it to a king from ancient times named Solomon. Could this be that ring?

A shiver ran across his chest, and Sassan's grip on the tongs loosened. The ring dropped onto the rug.

Sassan bent down. The tongs being cumbersome, he touched the ring with a fingertip and then two. It was cool. He picked it up and examined it.

There was no way to tell if this was the ring, *the seal* King Solomon had used to enslave the djinn nation.

The ring was made for a king, he told himself.

Perhaps he was meant to give the ring to the emperor, let him wear and deal with the djinn-and-daevas problem. The idea had considerable appeal. But to give the ring to the emperor would be to admit failure. It might even suggest to others that God favoured the emperor over His own high magus.

Sassan shook his head.

Now you're being paranoid. If that were true, why was the ring delivered to you? You asked for a sign, not a means of controlling the djinn. Maybe this ring is just that, a sign.

There was only one way to find out. Sassan held the ring over the middle finger of his trembling right hand. He took a deep breath and then slid it over his finger.

Sassan counts six steps, each carrying him closer to a throne draped in purple silk and canopied. A carved wooden eagle perches on top of the throne. The carving is so intricate, exquisite, it is as if a real eagle looks down at him. He turns and sits. Beneath the steps is a hall filled with men, women and children. He sees the red flames around their eyes. Sassan raises his right hand. At the sight of the ring, the djinn drop to their knees.

Their voices, the sound of a dry thunderstorm, say as one, 'Command us, Bearer of the Seal.'

Sassan exhaled, opened his eyes and found himself back inside his tent.

He clamped a hand to his mouth to smother a giggle. Tears blurred his vision as he knelt.

'Thank you, God. Thank you, God. Thank you, God.'

He heaved himself up, his legs shaky and his skin coated with sweat.

A thought hammered into him and made him stagger.

Sassan regained his balance and steadied his breathing. He headed for the tent's exit but then stopped when he remembered the golden arrow, the sabaoth's arrow. He grabbed it, knocking the amphora of diluted poppy juice onto the floor, and dashed outside.

Inside the operations tent, General Afacan's senior staff had joined him. He and the rest of his officers stood to attention. Sassan wondered what he must have looked like, because the general regarded him with concern more than surprise.

'I'm sorry to interrupt, General,' he said, then realised he was wheezing. Sassan wanted to laugh, jump, shout with joy. He puffed out his chest and raised his chin. 'I want you to cancel my last order and postpone the executions.'

11

E mad looked up to see Shephatiah waiting for him at the top of the rocky hill. The cool morning breeze did nothing to stop sweat coating his face. His thighs and calves burned from the climb, causing Emad's feet to drag for the final few steps.

'Are you all right, Your Highness?' Shephatiah said.

Emad neither felt nor looked all right.

'I'm just getting old, lad.'

The djinni bent his head back to take in the dark-grey fort. A mosaic of different-sized rocks, not brick, formed its high walls.

'I could have raised a portal instead of you climbing the stairs,' Shephatiah said.

One corner of Emad's mouth rose. The lad had no idea.

'If you had, our heads would have left our shoulders before we could step through there.' He pointed at the giant double doors and their open wicket gate. 'Our hosts don't like surprises. They like to know they have visitors before they arrive.'

'I see,' Shephatiah said.

Emad didn't think so.

'Come on,' he said. 'We don't want to keep our hosts waiting.'

Shephatiah's loud intake of breath made Emad smile.

Beyond the wicket gate, a garden filled the courtyard, a white marble fountain at its centre. Their boots crunched on pea-sized gravel as they moved deeper into the centre of the two-storey fort. Above them, the balconies appeared empty, but Emad knew they were being watched.

Rose bushes filled the garden. The blooms' scent and their jewel-like colours—coral, lapis and ruby—erupted from among the waxy green leaves.

'Remember, lad,' Emad whispered, 'don't move and don't speak unless spoken to.'

'Yes, Your Highness.'

Emad heard Shephatiah's step falter. He hadn't meant to scare the boy, although it was best to be careful in such a dangerous place.

Emad skirted the fountain, Shephatiah close behind. He found the patter of water increased his heart rate and didn't calm it. When he spotted her, the hood of her red robe pulled over her head, he held out a halting hand.

'Stay here,' he said. 'Keep your hands together so they know you're not weaving magic.'

The figure in the robe held a basket in one hand. She put it down and, using the knife in the other, deadheaded a spent rose.

As Emad approached, he saw she had cut her thumb where she'd held the rose's stalk.

'I've lost nearly all sensation in them,' she said, without looking up.

'The roses are as beautiful as the last time I was here, Tarana. I don't remember seeing those blue ones, though.'

She looked up, the hood sliding from her face.

Tarana's white hair hung in scattered wisps from her balding pate. The disease had eaten away all of her nose, a leather patch covering an area just above the centre of her face. The vermillion border of her upper lip had also disappeared.

Emad bent forward and kissed each cheek.

'Still unflappable,' Tarana said, and chuckled.

Emad shook his head.

'I still see the little girl who sat with me the first time I was here. You showed me you could crack walnuts with your hands.'

Tarana pulled the hood over her head.

'You didn't come here to reminisce, djinni,' she said, her voice gruff.

She'd seen his eyes. Tarana had given him the opening he needed.

'If I were still a djinni, this would be a social visit.'

Tarana dropped the rose head into the basket. She then reached forward and cut off another spent rose with an expert flick. Emad tried not to think about how her knife and hands had done the same to throats.

'Zafran is away,' she said. 'Nowadays, he runs the clan and conducts clan business.'

So, the son had followed in his mother's and grandfather's footsteps. Tarana had wanted her son to experience the world and those who peopled it. Zafran had crewed for Emad for five years and could have, one day, made an outstanding captain.

'It's advice I need, Tarana, and you're the wisest woman I know in your line of business.'

Beneath her hood, Tarana shook her head.

'That's because I'm the *only* woman in the business.' She looked up at him, her eyes slits. 'What advice do you need, old friend?'

Emad explained the djinn's and daevas' dilemma. Tarana listened and continued to deadhead the bush in front of her. When Emad had finished, she stood with the edge of her blade poised over a spent rose.

'Hmm,' she said, the sound like a purr. 'The high magus, you say. And there must be no suggestion the djinn are behind his death. It will be a very dangerous and very expensive undertaking, Emad. And if he should have this seal you mentioned, retrieving it will certainly raise suspicion.'

He had to agree.

'That's why I'm here. If what I need is possible, you're the only one with the experience and the resources to make it happen.'

Tarana still hadn't deadheaded the spent rose.

'In all the years I've known you, Emad, I've never heard you so desperate. What you require of the clan will take planning, and resources gathered from far and wide. What you ask for won't happen overnight.'

Emad clenched a fist and tried to hide his disappointment.

She hasn't said it can't be done.

'How long will you need?'

'Zafran returns this evening. He has no immediate contracts that require his attention.' She gazed at him, although her mind looked as if it were somewhere else. 'You were a good friend to my father, and you've been a good friend to me and to my son. I and the clan have no love of the empire. We will help you, Emad, but what you require will take a week to arrange.'

When she'd finished talking, Tarana deadheaded the spent rose with an expert flick of her knife.

It wasn't as soon as he'd wanted, but Emad took comfort knowing that Tarana considered Sassan's murder and the retrieval of the seal feasible.

'Thank you,' he said.

Tarana dropped the spent rose and then the knife into the basket.

'Don't thank me yet,' she said. 'We haven't discussed the price.'

12

Sassan entered the operations tent and found General Afacan waiting for him.

'Think, speak and act well, High Magus.'

'Think, speak and act well, General.'

Sassan noticed how the general stared at the sabaoth's arrow he held, or was it the signet ring he wore? He held up the seal so the general could get a better look.

'I have received another gift from the sabaoth,' he declared.

The general's gaze remained inscrutable.

He doesn't have a clue what this is and what it can do. The excitement he'd entered the tent with fizzled out.

'Have arrangements been made, General?' he said, the question close to a growl.

The general bowed.

'They have, High Magus. I had five prisoners transferred to a separate tent, along with the two volunteers you requested.'

'Excellent,' Sassan said. He turned and made to leave.

'High Magus.'

His back to the general, Sassan glowered. He faced General Afacan again.

'Yes, General?'

Afacan stood with his hands behind his back.

'Please tell me what two of my men have volunteered for.'

Just like the general to be protective towards his guardsmen.

'I want the daevas to raise a portal. We need to reach the coast and locate Baka fast. Portals will save the army time.'

The general's eyes moved down and to his right at the news.

'Are you expecting my men to provide auric energy to the daevas?' he said.

'Precisely.'

The general shook his head.

'With respect, High Magus, my men are trained to fight. They accept they may die in battle. But to surrender their auric energy to a daeva—I cannot allow you to use them in this way.'

This was unexpected.

'They won't come to any harm, I assure you, General. They'll feel tired afterwards. A meal and some rest will see them right again. If I can't use them, we'll face weeks of marching.' He held up the ring again. 'God has given me the means of controlling the daevas. I've asked for the older daevas first. Their frailty will make it harder for them to resist. They will have no choice but to follow my commands. I just need a little auric energy to test the seal and to understand how much influence I have over the daevas.'

The general lowered his eyes. He then fixed Sassan with a stare.

'Very well, High Magus. If, however, my men appear to be in any danger, I'll order them to leave the tent.'

Sassan wanted to poke the general with the tip of his arrow. What were two men if the other three thousand didn't have to slog their way across weeks of desert?

'I understand, General,' he said. He pointed at the tent's exit. 'Shall we?'

Sassan found five manacled male daevas seated on the floor

at the back of the prisoners' tent. The two volunteer guardsmen recognised the general and stood to attention.

Four of the daevas looked ancient—one of them had fallen asleep. The fifth, the youngest looking, Sassan wagged a finger at.

'Come here,' he said. The daevas looked among themselves, unsure which of them he'd referred to you. Sassan took a step closer. 'You,' he said, and pointed.

The daeva rose, his steps wary.

'Come now,' Sassan said, sounding cheerful. 'I won't hurt you.' He indicated the daeva should stop. 'Just there—good.' He signalled a guardsman to remove the daeva's manacles. Without iron touching his skin, the daeva straightened. Sassan said, 'What's your name?'

The daeva looked across at the others. One of the daevas nodded.

'Ninib, High Magus.'

Sassan hesitated. Should he show the daeva the ring, or would the seal compel the daeva to follow his commands?

'Ninib, I want you to ask a guardsman over there to give you a little of their auric energy. I want you to raise a portal for me.'

Ninib's jaw dropped.

'A portal?'

Sassan nodded and smiled.

'That's right.'

Sassan glanced over his shoulder at the guardsmen. They looked as bemused as the daeva. One guardsman looked at the general.

Sassan tightened his grip on the sabaoth's arrow.

'You can leave at any time,' he said. 'If either of you are any in danger, I will stop this.'

The general nodded his confirmation to the guardsmen.

'Right, now we have that sorted,' Sassan said, 'Ninib, ask a guardsman for some of their auric energy.'

Ninib looked again at the other daevas. Two of them

shrugged. Ninib took a deep breath and faced the guardsman who'd unshackled him.

'Er, sir, may I have some of your auric energy, please?'

The guardsman cast a sideways glance at the general, pushed his shoulders back and gave the daeva a quick nod.

Ninib closed his eyes. He took several breaths before he opened them. He faced Sassan.

'Do you have the coordinates for the destination window, High Magus?'

A shiver made Sassan's chest tighten.

'Open a destination window to Baka.'

Ninib shook his head.

'I don't have those coordinates, High Magus.'

The daeva could be telling the truth or lying. Sassan had no way of telling. He took a step closer to Ninib and held up his hand so he could see the seal.

Blood drained from the daeva's face. His brow furrowed and his eyes bulged.

Sassan saw his chance.

'Raise a portal to Baka.'

Ninib snapped to attention. All signs of fear had disappeared. The incantation sounded like a hiss as he worked his hands to weave a destination window. A boarding window followed. They fused, dark-green light circling the portal's border.

Sassan saw a forest of evergreens blanketing the slope of a mountain. Water foamed as it churned through rapids at the mountain's base.

'What's that?' Sassan said. 'I asked you to raise a portal to Baka. You're supposed to show me a city by the sea.'

As if a guardsman, Ninib stood to attention. His eyes remained fixed on some distant point.

'I do not know where Baka is. The portal leads to Laka,' he said.

Sassan shook his head. Compelled, the daeva had produced

an approximation of Sassan's request. Maybe Ninib didn't know Baka's whereabouts. His initial elation at using the seal on the daeva waned. What use was it if only the djinn had Baka's location? He marched over to the four other daevas and waved the ring at them. Three cowered; the fourth still slept.

'Do any of you know the whereabouts of Baka? It's on the edge of the Caspas satrapy and the Casperan Sea.'

Three of the daevas sat up and shook their heads. The fourth opened his rheumy eyes, his head and cheeks a fuzz of white stubble. He moved his lips. No sound escaped his toothless mouth.

Sassan bent down. Their eyes met, and Sassan wanted to look away.

'Do you know where it is?'

The daeva grinned.

'My father's old, High Magus,' Ninib said. 'Nowadays, he's very forgetful.'

Sassan ignored Ninib. This daeva had opened his eyes at the mention of Baka. Senile or not, he knew something.

'What's your name?'

'Pudil,' the daeva said. He looked as if the question had woken him from a dream. 'Who are you? Why are you holding a gold arrow?'

Sassan felt the general's eyes on him. He recalled Afacan's inscrutable stare when he'd shown him the seal.

You're getting desperate if you think this daeva can help you.

'My name is Sassan. Pudil, you're here to help me find a city called Baka. Can you help me?'

Pudil's brow creased. His eyes, however, never left Sassan's.

'I've heard the name. I'm getting forgetful, though. Could you spare some auric energy to help me remember, young man?'

Sassan stood up. He wasn't falling for such trickery.

'Pudil,' he said, compelling the daeva, 'tell me where Baka is.'

The daeva flopped onto his back and squealed. The three

other daevas shuffled back to put some distance between Pudil and them.

'Aaaiii! Stop it. It hurts! It hurts! Don't use that thing on me.'

Sassan backed away. Pudil stopped screaming. Sassan turned to Ninib.

'What's wrong with him?'

Ninib gazed at Pudil. His expression conveyed both sympathy and resignation. Sassan recognised hate in the daeva's eyes when he answered.

'It's like he said, he needs auric energy. You can't compel us when we have little or no auric energy for magic.'

'High Magus.'

Sassan turned and faced General Afacan.

'A word, High Magus, please.'

Sassan nodded. He knew what the general would say before he joined him.

'I won't let my men consent to giving this daeva any of their auric energy.'

Sassan nodded. Although eager to get at least the coordinates for a destination window—he could compel a different daeva to raise a portal another time—there was no telling how much auric energy Pudil would take.

'I understand,' Sassan said. He wracked his brain for a way to control the amount of energy the daeva drew. Could he use the seal to control the daeva and prevent him from taking more than he—

Of course, the seal!

It contained the auric energy King Solomon had taken from the djinn. He just needed to return a small amount to Pudil.

'Don't worry, General,' Sassan said. 'I have an idea.'

Sassan glanced at Pudil. The idea made sense. It was a good one, and it avoided putting the general's guardsmen in unnecessary danger. But how was he meant to release the energy the seal contained and ensure Pudil received it?

Pudil lay rocking from side to side. His shoulders shook with each sob.

God, please show me how to use your gift.

Sassan waited, but no vision, no images, came. Perhaps his learning how to use the ring was another of God's tests. Conscious of the general, his guardsmen and the daevas watching him, Sassan settled on an idea founded on nothing more than a hunch.

'Remove his manacles,' he told the guardsmen.

The daeva quietened and stopped rocking after being unshackled.

'Pudil,' Sassan said, then waved the daeva over. 'Come here. I have the auric energy you need.' He held up the ring.

Hunger crossed all four daevas' faces. Pudil didn't stand but crawled on all fours, his toothless mouth open, the tip of his tongue wetting his lower lip.

Sassan quivered with revulsion.

Pudil stopped in front of Sassan. He didn't stand but sat on his knees. His head jerked.

Sassan held out the ring. Pudil's mouth remained open. His eyes shone as he raised a hand, the fingers curled except for the index finger. Sassan held his breath, unsure if this was the right thing to do.

Pudil's fingertip brushed the ring's seal. His touch was so brief and light, Sassan wondered if he should tell the daeva to touch it again.

The daeva's head-jerking stopped. Pudil bowed, his shoulders rising and falling with every breath. Sassan glanced to his left, making sure both guardsmen remained alert.

Pudil raised his head. The red flames circling his irises made his eyes shine. Pudil stood. The white stubble dotting his pate and face had turned grizzled, and Sassan saw teeth when the daeva smiled.

Sassan felt his chest swell—he'd restored Pudil's auric energy to him.

'Do you know where Baka is? Do you have its coordinates?'

Pudil opened his mouth. His head flopped back, and he held his arms out from his sides.

'More,' the daeva said.

Sassan dropped his right hand and covered it with his left.

'Give me the coordinates to Baka, Pudil. I order you to.'

The daeva's head lolled forward, his nose wrinkled and his teeth gritted. Pudil's eyes became fiery red beads.

'Give me *more.*'

Sassan hid his right hand behind his back.

'High Magus'—it was the general—'I think you should leave.'

Was this the daeva madness? Was that why he couldn't compel Pudil?

'Give me the coordinates first, Pudil. Then I'll give you more.'

The daeva lurched forward and tried to grab Sassan.

'Give it to—' Pudil stopped mid-sentence.

With each word, red flames had burst from his mouth. The bulging veins on his neck and temples glowed as if fire and not blood flowed through them. Pudil held up his hands. The veins on the backs of them and his nail beds glowed. 'Too much,' he said, belching flames. 'Too much.'

'Do something,' Ninib said, the two guardsmen restraining him. 'You're killing my father.'

'Get those daevas out of here,' Sassan heard the general shout.

In front of him, Pudil's tunic had caught fire, the tall flames licking the tent's roof. The heat emanating from the daeva forced Sassan back. He held out the ring and imagined the surplus auric energy inside Pudil being sucked back into the seal.

The flames shortened for a breath and then erupted, brighter and hotter now.

He'd made it worse.

The old daeva's knees buckled, the flames surrounding him forming a fiery shaft that blew a hole in the canvas above.

'High Magus, we have to get out.'

General Afacan held his shoulders and dragged him away from the wall of heat. He nodded to the general.

Sassan stopped at the tent flaps and looked back. There was no sign of the daeva within the column of fire.

Outside, Sassan shook off the general's grip, then stared at the burning tent.

'The daevas don't know where Baka is, and the shoreline of the Caspas satrapy is vast,' he said as much to himself as the general. Sassan faced Afacan. His hands shook as much from shock as humiliation at his handling of this whole affair. He had to master the seal to save further embarrassment. 'Prepare another tent, General. I want a family this time. If the daevas can't tell me where Baka is, they'll tell me where the djinn live. Once I have the coordinates for that location, we'll capture a djinni, and then he or she will tell me where to find Baka.'

13

Zana watched as Father helped two daevas wedge a beam against a wall. This beam, along with the others, Father had explained to Zana, would support the wall while he used magic to clear away the sand beneath it. With the sand gone, he'd reinforce it with a separate incantation.

Father looked busy, which made Zana think he wouldn't appreciate being interrupted. He'd tried to speak to him last night and again this morning. Last night, Mother had seemed worried about something. It kept her and Father talking past Zana's bedtime. And before he and Father left for Iram this morning, both of his foster parents seemed preoccupied, even worried.

Zana glanced up and gauged the sun's position. If he were to meet Vul at the foot of the mountain, he'd have to leave now.

Father would understand, Zana told himself. *Father probably underwent lots of tests before becoming a warrior.*

The thought didn't reassure him. As Zana backed away and then strode off towards Baka's west wall and the city's entrance, it was as if something had changed. He never did anything without first seeking permission.

Vul's test, the Cross Scar pride's test, was difficult but not dangerous. By taking it without his foster parents' permission, he was about to cross a line that would change him and his relationship with Mother and Father.

Zana never felt so alone as he exited the city and turned left for the southernmost mountain.

Vul waited for him and so did Nahrian. They were both human and dressed in pale-brown robes that made them blend into their surroundings. Vul carried a waterskin and cloth bag, both of their straps slung over his shoulder. Zana thought Nahrian looked pleased to see him and a little relieved. As a human, Vul stood a head taller than Father. Vul looked bored. He turned without acknowledging Zana's nod and led the way.

Nahrian walked alongside Zana.

'When you get to the shelf, don't stand or sit—you must lie down,' Nahrian said, her voice a whisper. 'And stare at your nose, but don't close your eyes; otherwise, you risk falling asleep and moving.'

Since yesterday's meeting, Zana had looked for ways to ask his foster parents for permission to take the test but not what he'd have to do to pass it.

'Thank you,' he said to Nahrian. 'Is that how you did?'

Nahrian nodded.

'It's what my mother taught me.' She drew closer so her hip brushed his shoulder. 'The bowl of water Vul places in front of you, while it's a temptation, will keep you cool. If you remember that, you won't be so tempted to drink it.'

He thanked her again.

A hollowness occupied his chest as he'd left Baka. Nahrian's help filled some of the emptiness.

They wound their way around the mountain edge in silence. Vul stopped, pressed a rock to reveal a concealed entrance. Sunlight penetrated the shadows beyond the opening and lit stairs.

'This is your last chance,' Vul said, staring down his nose at Zana. 'The test begins the moment you enter the cave. If you fail, the manticore prides will shun you. If you turn back now, only the Cross Scar pride will know you're a coward.'

You idiot, Zana thought.

He'd never thought to ask what would happen if he failed the test.

Zana caught Vul smirking. Had he walked into a trap?

'Vul,' Nahrian said, 'that last bit isn't part of the test.' She knelt and faced Zana. 'We're all told the prides will shun us.' She scowled at her brother and then shook her head. 'You're not a coward. I heard about how you protected Roshan in Derbicca.' She rose and stepped away from him. 'Vul will go with you and oversee the test. My brother can be very rude, but he's honest and fair.'

Vul didn't respond. He turned and disappeared into the cave.

'Good luck,' Nahrian said.

Zana thanked her a third time. She was right: he wasn't a coward. He turned and entered the cave.

Inside, Zana found himself climbing a staircase that spiralled its way into the mountain. Firestones sunk into the rock just above each hewn step lit their way.

'Your birth mother was the leader of a pride,' Vul said as he climbed ahead of Zana. 'She was old when you were born. You were the runt of the litter and the only one of three cubs to survive birth.'

Zana halted on the steps. Yesterday, Vul had mentioned he could see the past and the future. Nahrian had told him her brother was honest and fair. Then what he was saying was the truth. Vul continued to climb and talk, his voice monotone, as if recalling a list of facts. Zana continued up the stairs.

'You were a three-year-old when a younger lioness from another pride, a larger pride, challenged your mother's leadership. Your mother lost the challenge, and you were both cast out. The two of you wandered from mountain to mountain, your mother hoping a pride took both of you in. But prides don't adopt cubs. And a pride will only let you join it if you can prove your value to it. Your mother's age and your age made you both a burden.

'For a year, your mother hunted and kept you both alive. Most leaders die within months of being deposed, but you gave her purpose. She protected you and taught you the importance of protecting the pride—even a pride of two.

'One evening, the pair of you stumbled upon a circus. While your mother saw an opportunity to steal food, the sounds and the lights captivated you. Your mother shifted into human shape, pulled on her robe and went off to get you both some food. You, Zana, lacked the discipline to remain where you promised your mother you'd wait. You wanted to take a closer look at those lights and search for the source of those sounds.

'When your mother returned, empty-handed, she found you gone. She searched and searched. By morning, the circus had packed and left. She realised you must have wandered into it, which meant you'd been captured, killed or both. Either way, she was too weak to follow the circus. Her heart broke. She lay down, closed her eyes and died.'

Zana tried to remember as he climbed and listened to Vul's dry voice. Nothing came to him. He couldn't dispute any of what Vul had said. Zana wept for the bereft lioness, for the mother whose cub abandoned her.

By the time they reached the top of the stairs and the shelf of rock overlooking the desert, Zana's emotions had swung from sadness to anger.

'Why did you tell me that?' he said.

Vul placed a bowl close to the shelf's edge. After he'd filled it with water from the waterskin, he folded his arms.

'Do your foster parents know you're here?'

Zana sat.

73

'What does that have to do with what you told me?'

Vul pointed at a space behind the bowl.

'This is where you sit. You must not move, and you must not drink. You may drink the water, but you will fail the test.'

Zana stood and approached the spot. He lay down as Nahrian had told him to. He stared up at Vul and stuck out his chin.

'You still haven't answered my question,' he said. 'Why did you tell me those things?'

Vul raised an eyebrow.

'You broke your promise to your mother, and you abandoned her. And now, by being up here with me, you're doing the same to your foster parents. I want you to know who you are, Zana. I want to protect my pride from you, and I want to protect you from yourself.' He turned his back on Zana and, with a hand shading his eyes, looked up. Vul turned. 'It's noon. If you wish to take the test, we begin now.'

14

Seated so close to Navid, Emad felt self-conscious.

Four of them, Yesfir, Fiqitush, Navid and Emad, sat in the audience chamber and stared at the destination window Fiqitush had woven. Their eyes never wandered from one tent among a cluster of seven. An hour earlier, they'd observed the daeva prisoners being marched out of Arshak, through the high magus's arc-shaped encampment and to the tents pitched behind it. Half an hour before, the high magus had entered a tent.

'Couldn't we move the destination window closer?' Navid said.

Emad still reeled from his brother's news. Shafira had died giving birth to twins. He'd been a father for eighteen years. Was he supposed to be grateful for being spared such news until now?

He still cringed at how he'd treated Roshan back in Derbicca. How was he supposed to tell her he was her father? And what about Navid? He couldn't say anything to either of them until they'd seen him in a better light. All they knew of him was his cantankerousness and stubbornness, a stubbornness that had gotten Aeshma killed.

'There are magi in the camp,' Fiqitush said, addressing Navid's question. 'If I move the window any closer, even though they can't see it, they might detect the Core power used to weave it.'

Emad took a deep breath, touched his bracelet and felt for the unique vibration his brother had shown him was Roshan's. He exhaled with relief. Her leaving without warning had alarmed everyone and left them all on edge. From her message to Navid, he and Fiqitush were sure she'd left with the sabaoth, Manah. From what Fiqitush had told him about her and from what he'd heard the others say, he knew Roshan had a good heart. Everything she did was with the best of intentions. Although he hardly knew her, he found himself worried about her. People with good hearts could be easily led.

'Is that smoke?' Yesfir said.

Emad looked up from his bracelet. Like everyone else, he bent forward.

Yesfir was right. Smoke drifted from the tent's entrance. The top of one sloping side blackened.

'What is going on in there?' his brother said.

A soldier emerged from the tent. He led a daeva out at sword point. The two soldiers on guard outside ran into the tent. They and another soldier pulled out three manacled daevas. The last to exit the tent, now an inferno, were the high magus and another soldier Fiqitush identified as General Afacan.

The soldiers, the daevas and the high magus stood nearby as the fire burned a hole in the tent's canvas. A column of flame swayed, shrank and then went out. The flame's source collapsed and shattered into several charred pieces.

Emad rubbed his chin.

'I counted five daevas enter that tent,' he said. 'Where's the fifth?'

From the looks exchanged, they all agreed they'd just witnessed the fifth daeva fall.

'The red flames suggest djinn magic,' Emad said. 'What we just saw might be the work of the seal.'

'We can't be sure,' Fiqitush said.

Emad understood how important the seal had been to his brother. News that Armaiti had taken it had been devastating enough. Sassan having it and using it on a daeva was beyond anything his brother could have imagined. No wonder Fiqitush refused his suggestion.

'It doesn't matter if it is or isn't the seal,' Emad said. 'Djinn and daevas don't catch fire, much less burn. If we're to know what we're up against, we have to risk a magus detecting our window and take a closer look. If we're quick enough, they won't be able to learn our coordinates from its signature.'

Navid answered instead of Fiqitush.

'I'll go. I've been practising my shape-shifting. I'll enter the camp as a rat.'

'Absolutely not,' Emad said. 'Nothing doing.'

Navid stared at him, confusion framing his face.

So much for his son seeing him in a better light.

Fiqitush frowned at Emad and then turned his attention to Navid.

'Are you sure? You'll go in without domes of protection or invisibility.'

Navid nodded, and Emad wanted to wring the young man's neck.

Yesfir sat up. She glanced at Fiqitush first and then pointed.

'There to the left of the camp,' she said. 'See those outcrops. They're far enough away for a portal to go undetected. You can change into a rat behind the tallest one and then make your way over to the tents with the daevas inside.'

Emad hated the plan.

'How's he supposed to get back?' he said.

'Good point, Uncle,' Yesfir said. 'I'll leave a destination

window open. As soon as I see Navid reach that outcrop furthest from the camp, I'll raise a portal and collect him.'

'Good,' Fiqitush said, before Emad could protest. 'Emad and I will keep watch and wait for things to settle before Navid leaves for Arshak.' He looked at Navid. 'Are you certain you've mastered your ability to shift, Navid? You've only had this skill three days.'

His son nodded, and Emad gave an inward groan.

'Good,' Fiqitush continued. 'Find the daevas inside the tent with the high magus and find out what happened.' Fiqitush raised a hand. 'But, at the first sign of danger, get out of there and return to those rocks. I don't want you adding to the worries I already have about your sister. Am I understood, young man?'

'Yes, Your Majesty,' Navid said, and bowed.

The corners of Fiqitush's lips rose.

'Good, then I suggest you and Yesfir get some lunch and discuss how you'll work together. Meanwhile, my brother and I will keep an eye on the camp.'

Yesfir and Navid left, the door to the audience chamber closing behind them.

Fiqitush shook his head and stood.

'Don't you dare, Emad,' he said. 'Don't you dare tell me Navid's your son and that I've just put him into danger.' His brother's eyes turned to slits. 'Who do you think has watched over the twins since they were born, made sure no one at the high temple discovered Roshan's djinn-like abilities? They're old enough to decide for themselves, and they're not Aeshma—they don't need fathering.'

The truth behind his brother's words felt like a punch to the gut. He shook his head.

'At least I didn't have them live as orphans, kidnap them and turn poor Navid into a rat.'

Fiqitush nodded.

'I would have loved for Roshan and Navid to live among family in Iram. But their mother wanted them to live as humans.

If, as they grew older, their eyes didn't change colour, being magi meant giving them a good start in life.'

After the difficult lesson she'd learned about herself, Emad understood the reasoning behind Shafira's wish. He held up his hands in surrender.

'You told me I was their father, Fiqitush. What am I supposed to do, knowing that? If I'm not supposed to protect them and father them, what should I do?'

Fiqitush crossed the space between them and took Emad by the shoulders.

'As soon as you get the chance, tell them who you are, and then let them decide, brother.'

15

N avid entered the audience chamber with Yesfir. Earlier, Yesfir had insisted he eat something before leaving for Arshak. The little rice and goat meat he'd eaten felt like sand in his stomach. After seeing the tent catch fire, like everyone else, he wanted to know what Sassan was up to and if the high magus had Solomon's seal. The thought of roaming around a camp filled with three thousand guardsmen made him queasy.

He spotted the destination window first and then saw the king and his brother watching events play out in Arshak. He felt the prince's eyes on him as he approached. The daeva hardly knew him. So, why did he behave as if he held some authority over him?

He is a prince, he said to himself. *Maybe he thinks he can decide for me.*

The king pointed at a new tent erected ten paces to the right of the incinerated one.

'Half an hour before, guardsmen led a couple and their son into that tent,' the king said. His attention remained fixed on the window. 'The high magus entered soon after.' He faced Navid.

'Get as close as you can and find out what's going on in there. Remember, the moment you think you're in danger, return to the taller of these two outcrops.'

The king adjusted the destination window by tilting it down and to the left. Navid saw two jagged islands of sandstone, the one closest to the encampment longer than the furthest but too short for anyone to hide behind. Navid estimated the first outcrop was thirty paces from the encampment and the second twenty more. If anyone saw him, his dark-brown fur would stand out against the exposed rock and sand.

Navid acknowledged the king with a nod.

Yesfir handed him a shoulder bag for his clothes and a waterskin. She then raised a portal.

'Good luck,' the prince said.

'Thank you,' Navid replied, and then stepped through.

His heart pounded as he stepped onto warm rock. It continued hammering inside his head as he unslung the waterskin and then undressed. The outcrop's shadow shielded him from the sun's rays. The surrounding ground was rocky and there was nowhere for him to bury the shoulder bag and waterskin.

That's the first and only setback, he told himself.

He crouched, tensed and imagined himself as a rat. The change wasn't so much painful as disorientating. Arms became legs, a nose became a snout, palms were pads, sunlight no longer touched bare skin but fur, and it felt as if the length of his spine had doubled. Navid curled his tail in when it touched the warm rock beneath. Water from his human body left the rock pockmarked with droplets.

If I can't make it back to the outcrop, Navid wondered, *will there be sufficient water in the surrounding air for me to shift back again?* He'd been practising indoors and not under direct sunlight. *You ass. Next time, think things through before you volunteer yourself.*

For fear of being scalded, Navid shook off the water

covering his fur, then scurried around the edge of the rock. He located the second, shorter outcrop and sprinted towards it. The level rocky surface, though hot, helped him to maintain a fast pace.

At the second outcrop, he took his time edging around it, keeping his eyes peeled for any movement along the camp's outskirts. He made out three men, one of them oiling his unstrung bow and the other two trimming their arrows' fletchings.

This time, his route would have to be circuitous, one that involved him running between outcrops tall enough to hide him. His eyesight and lack of height made it difficult to see where the terrain grew sandier and left him exposed.

The sun burned his back, and standing on rock was equally unpleasant. He had to move or risk being roasted alive.

Navid dashed between the jutting rock, his route zigzagging from left to right. As expected, the rock surrendered to sand. Navid slowed to avoid slipping on the surface, his claws providing grip.

He located the tent from the cries coming from inside. It sounded to Navid as if a male daeva were being tortured. Navid slowed and took cover beneath the corner of a tent facing the one the high magus had entered. Two guardsmen flanked its entrance. If he approached the tent head-on, they'd spot him.

Another flaw in the plan.

He scanned his surroundings, searching for a way to go around the guarded tent and sneak in through the back. A plan took shape when he saw how the tents housing the daevas had been erected with their entrances facing each other.

Navid ran back the way he came but stopped short of the three archers. Then he took a wide looping arc to his left and around the camp's perimeter, the tents forming it unguarded. Thirsty and hot, he swung back, narrowly avoiding a patrolling guardsman, and arrived behind the tents housing the prisoners.

The cries continued. Navid found the back of the tent and burrowed his way beneath the canvas.

The tent's interior was bare except for the three daevas and the high magus. The boy and his mother, both manacled, cowered in a far corner. Like the boy he'd met in Iram, Ehsan, this one couldn't have been over six years old.

High Magus Sassan stood over a kneeling daeva—the father. Sassan held a golden arrow in his left hand. He had curled his right hand into a fist and held it out a handspan from the daeva's face. Navid swallowed a squeak when he saw a ring on the middle finger of Sassan's right hand.

'Stop fighting the seal,' Sassan said, his brow glistening with sweat. 'Don't resist and the pain will stop.' The high magus levelled the ring at the daeva's bowed head. 'If you can't give me Baka's coordinates, tell me where the djinn live.'

Smoke rose from the daeva's shoulders, and Navid smelled burning flesh.

Navid's claws sank between the grains of sand as he clenched his front paws. Sassan's upper lip had curled back to reveal his teeth, and his eyes regarded the daeva as if he were prey.

Navid pushed himself further into the tent. He was ready to shape-shift and stop the high magus when Sassan dropped his arm.

The daeva panted while the high magus gazed at him.

'I'm impressed,' Sassan said. 'I didn't know daevas could resist Solomon's seal. Perhaps it has something to do with you no longer being a djinni.' He wiped the sweat from his forehead with his tunic's cuff. 'I don't have a djinni to test my theory. But that will change, because one of you will tell me where the djinn are hiding.' He pointed the golden arrow at the boy. 'This morning, I returned some auric energy to a daeva. His name was Pudil. I'm still learning how the seal works. I returned too much energy to Pudil and'—Sassan shook his head—'the poor fellow burned to death. I thought fire couldn't hurt your people.' He pointed the ring at the boy. 'If you love your son, one of you will tell me where the djinn are hiding, or he will burn.'

Navid took a deep breath through his nose and relaxed all his muscles. Navid closed his eyes, unsure if the air inside the tent was humid enough for him to shift and not collapse from dehydration.

'Wait.'

Navid opened them.

The female daeva clambered to her feet, her arms still wrapped around her son.

'I'll tell you,' she said. 'Just don't hurt my son.'

'Shala,' her husband said. He'd shuffled around so he could look at her. Tears mingled with the sweat pouring from his face. 'You mustn't. He'll execute as all anyway. Please don't.'

The woman ignored her husband and fixed Sassan with a determined stare.

'The djinn live in a city called Iram,' she said. 'Swear by the Divine Light you won't harm my son, and I'll give you the coordinates.'

Sassan ignored the male daeva's cry of anguish.

'You have my word, madam.'

If you shape-shift and you can't stop the high magus, who will warn Iram?

It took all of Navid's willpower to back out of the tent. He retraced the route he'd taken. The three archers had their backs to him, which gave him the chance to take a more direct route to the short outcrop.

He ran as fast as he could, concentrating on the sunrays beating against his fur. Better that than remembering what he'd witnessed.

Halfway to the outcrop, Navid heard a *whoosh*. Before he could ask himself why he recognised the sound, something slid past his right side.

Navid heard cheers coming from the camp.

'I told you I saw a rat,' someone said.

Closer to the outcrop, he bounded forward and squeaked in pain. He somersaulted and landed on his back. An arrow passed over him and clattered against the rock. Navid bent forward to examine the pain's source. Blood seeped from his open hip. As if looking through another's eyes, he noted the deep cut and how the arrow had severed a ligament. His right hind leg was useless.

Another arrow struck the rock, this one closer.

Move!

He rolled onto his front and, ignoring how his leg dangled behind him, raced towards the outcrop. Instinct—human or rat —took over. Unwilling to make himself an easy target, he snaked the best he could without letting his damaged leg trip him. When he judged he was close enough, he leapt into the air and threw himself over the top of the outcrop.

Navid landed with a squeak. He'd torn more muscles in his injured thigh. He lay gasping in lungfuls of air and fought against blacking out.

Boos from the camp reached his ears. Those archers were using him for target practise.

He pushed himself onto his three good legs and pressed his left side against the rock. While he got his breath back, he tried to gauge the distance between this outcrop and the taller one where he'd left his clothes and the waterskin. Open ground lay left and right of him, leaving him exposed.

'Come out, ratty,' an archer shouted. 'Come out so we can skewer you.'

All three laughed.

If they knew he was hiding, then they'd either wait for him to emerge, or one of them would flush him out for the other two to shoot at.

You'll have to stay here and hope they get bored. If one of them comes over, then play dead. Run and an arrow will get you.

He liked the idea. It was a good one—until the coppery tang

of blood reached his nose. If he waited, he'd bleed to death and there'd be no need to play dead.

Everything that could go wrong had gone wrong.

Navid thought of the boy inside the tent with Sassan. He remembered the two sisters in Iram and how they'd giggled at the sight of Zana's teeth. And what about the boy with the tablet who'd drawn a picture of a manticore?

For their sakes, run for it.

Navid turned to face the second outcrop. He bowed his head as he readied to thrust forward with his one back leg.

Navid felt himself cupped between two hands. He recognised her scent before he saw her face.

Yesfir.

She pulled him to her breast and turned towards the tall outcrop.

A dome of invisibility, he thought, and then passed out.

16

The stone pillars blocked dawn's light, casting long shadows across the basin. Roshan sat in the shadow of what looked like a giant stalagmite. She shuffled sideways to catch the rays of the rising sun and warm her back.

Roshan examined the ten uncut diamonds she held. The warmth from the burning pile of charcoal offered little comfort during the cold and miserable night. Its oily fragrance smelled to Roshan like defeat.

Not one diamond had come from a piece of charcoal that hadn't scorched the surrounding lumps. She'd done as Manah had instructed and concentrated on what she wanted: an uncut diamond the size of the nail on her little finger. She had tried her best not to think about pressure and heat, leaving that to the sentient Domain power to figure out. If the Domain power had warned her, let her know her thoughts had strayed from the outcome she'd wanted, Roshan hadn't felt it.

Her inability to sense the wrongness of the magic she wove left her deflated. She kept going over Manah's words: *Whether or not you want to, you could destroy the world with a single thought.*

He'd said she was very dangerous, and from the burning pile of charcoal it was clear why.

Roshan threw the diamonds onto the fire, then straightened her tunic's collar against last night's chill.

'You've given up.'

Manah stood on the opposite side of the fire, his forehead crimped.

'The heat, I couldn't confine it,' she said.

The lamassu prodded the fire, separating the charcoal from the diamonds to study them.

'I had hoped for a little better,' he said. 'Did you try the second exercise?'

Roshan's shoulders tensed.

'So long as it just swam up and down the length of the trough, I managed to keep the water around the fish cool. If it changed direction suddenly, the poor thing died.'

Her explanation sounded like an excuse. It didn't matter. If she couldn't stop herself from burning more than one lump of charcoal or boiling a fish, what kind of harm might she inflict on the innocent every time she wove sabaoth magic?

'You've only been practising for one night,' Manah said. 'It took Yesfir two years to add to what you'd already learned as a novice and to teach you djinn magic. You're not making excuses, but you are expecting too much of yourself.'

Roshan relaxed a little.

'If you're suggesting it will take years before I can master sabaoth magic, how am I supposed to help the djinn and daevas? You said yourself, Armaiti has the seal and she'll use it against them. Can you speed up my learning or improve the accuracy of my thoughts?'

Manah scraped a cloven hoof against the rock.

'That's not what God sent me here to do.'

About to burst, Roshan took a deep breath to calm herself.

'If it's going to take me years'—she held out a hand and drew a circle around the fire—'what are we doing here? What's the point of me making diamonds and boiling fish?'

Manah smiled.

Is he enjoying himself? Roshan wondered.

'No djinn or human has ever had such a gift as yours, Roshan. God wants you to understand the nature of Domain power and the challenges you will face wielding sabaoth magic.'

Roshan raised her chin.

'Is that why you brought me here? Do you want me to stay here and keep out of the djinn's and daevas' way?' She shook her head. 'I can still weave human and djinn magic. I won't stay here and leave them to fight Armaiti on their own.'

She raised her arms to weave a destination window to Iram, then caught Manah smiling again.

'I never suggested such a thing,' he said. 'If I had, you wouldn't be able to channel energy to the likes of Yesfir and Behrouz.'

Roshan lowered her arms.

'What do you mean?'

'I mean, the energy you're channelling through the bracelet you're wearing only lasts a finite time in a djinni or a daeva. It needs to be renewed, and that's not something you can do from a great distance. If you continue to channel energy to all the djinn and daevas, you can't be this far away from them.'

In her dream, she hadn't just replenished Behrouz's and Yesfir's auric energy.

'I'm only one person. What would happen to my aura?'

Her question drew an approving nod from the lamassu.

'The sabaoth energy within your aura will draw Domain power and use it to channel your energy to the djinn and daevas. That same power will replenish your own aura. With time, however, your aura will consist mostly of sabaoth energy. Helping the djinn and daevas in this way won't harm you. When large numbers of them weave magic, you'll get tired, but it will only last for as long as they weave magic.'

Before she could ask him if the sabaoth energy filling her aura was the reason her skin had changed colour, he shook his head.

'You're here, Roshan, because God wants you to understand that, for now, the best way to help the djinn and daevas is to channel your auric energy to them. By all means, practise those exercises, but we both know Armaiti plans on using the seal. Restore their auric energy, and Armaiti won't have an easy fight on her hands.'

Manah's exercises, her attempt to emulate his skill with weaving sabaoth magic had showed how much she still had to learn. To Roshan, channelling energy was too passive. She wanted to fight alongside the djinn and daevas, not sit about while they drew auric energy through her bracelet.

Roshan glimpsed Daniyel's smile.

She straightened.

'Thank you, Manah,' she said. 'I understand now, and you're right.'

17

E mad picked at his food. Their early dinner in Fiqitush's chamber was a sombre affair. Both Fiqitush and Yesfir appeared as disinterested in their meal as he was in his. Only Behrouz had an appetite. With Roshan's sudden departure and Navid sleeping off his injury, the four of them were at a loss for what to do. Until Navid woke and told them what he'd witnessed in the encampment, Fiqitush didn't know what their options were.

Emad kept telling himself his worrying about the twins was irrational. Until yesterday, he hadn't known he was a father. Before then, and oblivious to their existence, he hadn't worried.

They're your flesh and blood, he told himself.

So was Aeshma.

He picked up his bowl and drank some water. A cold sweat crept across his forehead and down the back of his neck.

Were his concerns over the twins, his protectiveness towards them, because of what had happened to Aeshma?

There was a knock on the door.

'It's Roshan,' Yesfir said, with a broad smile.

The mood in the chamber lightened.

Fiqitush called, 'Come in.'

Embarrassed at failing to recognise his daughter's presence through his bracelet, Emad was the first to stand, but Yesfir beat him to the door and hugged Roshan before she could enter the room.

To Emad, it looked as if Roshan's return had lifted a weight from his brother.

Behrouz, his fingers still greasy, gave Roshan a one-armed hug. Emad noted how he and Fiqitush had expressed their relief at seeing her with only a smile.

To make room for Roshan, he and Fiqitush moved aside the bowls of rice and okra stew. Everyone sat.

'Where have you been?' Yesfir said.

Roshan shrugged.

'I have the coordinates, but I don't know. I left here yesterday afternoon, but it was dusk over there.'

Behrouz's hands dwarfed his finger bowl, forcing him to wash one hand at a time.

Because no one had asked, Emad said, 'Will you have to leave again?'

'No,' Roshan said, and shook her head. She described Manah's exercises, and then she explained the conclusion she'd arrived at, her way of helping the djinn and daevas. Roshan looked over at Fiqitush. 'We don't need the seal to defend ourselves.'

For a moment, Emad thought Fiqitush might crumple and pass out. His brother closed his eyes and rubbed the bridge of his nose. He took a deep breath, exhaled and then opened his tear-filled eyes. Not since their father's death had Emad seen his brother so emotional.

'Thank you, Roshan,' Fiqitush said. 'You've saved us.'

Fiqitush, you're as affectionate as a blade of kelp, Emad thought.

Yesfir came to Fiqitush's rescue.

'You said *maintain.* What does that mean?'

Emad listened to Roshan explain how the energy she'd restore to the djinn and daevas, like the auric energy he'd taken from Widow Sharo to reshape her daughter's nose, was finite. If a djinni wasn't wearing his bracelet, the energy would run out in a day or two. Emad didn't wait for someone else to ask.

'But you're one woman,' he said. 'There are around one hundred djinn and four hundred daevas. If you restore and replenish all of their auras, what happens to yours?'

Roshan smiled. She seemed grateful for his concern.

'Domain power, the power the sabaoth use for weaving magic, will replenish my aura. The only problem that could arise is I'll get tired if large numbers of daevas and djinn draw on my aura at the same time.'

Her answer reduced his concern by only half. He looked over at Fiqitush.

'Is there some way we could stop that from happening?' Emad said.

His brother did well to hide his disappointment from the others. Emad saw how Fiqitush dug his fingertips into his thigh. This wasn't the permanent solution the seal would have provided.

'We'll think of something,' Fiqitush said. 'Reviving their auric energy would allow the djinn and daevas to speed up Baka's reconstruction.' He held up a hand. 'But they'll work in shifts. That way, they won't all be weaving magic at once and tiring Roshan.'

Emad had seen the city with its breached walls that wouldn't stop a camel and northernmost watchtower sinking beneath sand. Its location proved its only redeeming feature: mountains flanked the city's north and south walls, while its east wall faced the sea.

'Baka requires so much work, Fiqitush. Wouldn't relocating the djinn and daevas to some far-off part of the world, like the place Roshan described, be a better solution than Baka?'

93

Before Fiqitush could answer, Emad heard a second knock on the door. This time, the door opened without permission. Shephatiah poked his head through the opening.

'Your Majesty,' he said, 'you asked me to let you know when Navid woke.'

Everyone stood, ready to leave for Navid's room.

Roshan looked confused.

'Don't worry,' he mouthed at her.

'There's, um, no need to go to him,' Shephatiah said. 'He's outside. Should I let him in?'

Emad rolled his eyes. He wanted to scold the djinni for his unnecessary formality.

'Of course, of course,' Fiqitush said.

Yesfir, again, was the first to hug the young man before he could make it through the door. When Navid made it into the chamber, Emad reached out and shook his hand.

'Good job,' he said.

Navid's handshake was firm.

'Thank you.'

Emad cursed himself for being as formal as his brother.

'How are you feeling?' Behrouz said. 'That arrow looked to have done some serious damage when Yesfir brought you in.'

Navid smiled at Roshan and sidled across the chamber to join her. Brother and sister hugged before sitting down.

'I don't know how it works,' Navid said. 'As soon as I changed back, the wound had healed.' His eyes fell on the bowls of rice and stew. He pointed at the food. 'I'm so hungry, I almost went to the kitchen instead of coming here.'

Emad sat down and let Yesfir spoon the contents of both bowls onto a clean plate and then handed it to Navid. Roshan stared at her brother's plate.

She hasn't eaten either.

'Are you hungry, Roshan?'

Before she could answer, Navid handed her his plate.

'The high magus has the coordinates for Iram,' Navid said.

Roshan choked on some rice. Navid rubbed her back.

'What does he plan on doing?' Emad said.

The others' questions drowned out his.

Fiqitush held up his hand for silence.

'Did I hear that correctly?' he said.

Navid nodded.

'I saw the high magus interrogating a daeva, using the seal.'

Emad felt sick. His brother's face turned white. And just when he thought it couldn't get worse, Navid described how Sassan had used the seal to extract coordinates for Iram. For now, Baka was safe because none of the daevas knew the city's location. If Sassan were to capture a djinni, he'd have Baka's coordinates and more.

After Navid had finished his report, Emad said, 'The high magus knows about Baka and Iram. If captures a djinni, he'll be able to raise portals. That means both cities are in danger.'

Everyone nodded.

Fiqitush pursed his lips and then opened them with a *smack*.

'We have to abandon Iram and accelerate Baka's reconstruction. We must start now, tonight.'

Emad guessed that Fiqitush wanted to keep the djinn and daevas together, because he saw strength in numbers. But with Baka in such a dilapidated state, Emad wondered why his brother was so fixated with the city. To avoid undermining his brother's authority, he'd have to wait until after everyone had left to ask.

Roshan took the plate from her brother, her fingers poised to roll some rice and stew into a ball.

'What about the prisoners in Arshak?' she said. 'We can't leave them with the high magus. Who knows what he'll do to them and what else he'll learn?'

Things were getting complicated. Emad watched as brother and sister took turns to eat the remaining food. With the threats to Iram and Baka, and over thirty daevas in need of rescue, Fiqitush would call on the twins for help again.

Look at them, he said to himself. *They've managed without parents this long. We all have a lot to worry about. Now wouldn't be the best time to tell them.*

Navid raised his hand.

'What is it?' Fiqitush said.

'There's something I saw that might be important.' He waited until Fiqitush nodded for him to continue. 'The daeva being interrogated looked to be resisting the seal. By the time I'd arrived, the seal had badly burned him, but he still didn't talk. His wife surrendered Iram's coordinates because the high magus threatened to set their son alight.'

Behrouz pulled off his bracelet. The red flames around his eyes flickered.

'I'll go to Arshak as a daeva,' he said.

Yesfir reached for her bracelet.

'No,' Fiqitush said. He scanned the room's walls and then its ceiling. 'For all we know, Armaiti could be in here, listening to us. If she is, we'll have to keep things simple and create a plan that allows for some improvising during its execution. You, Yesfir, must stay here and keep an eye on what's going on in Arshak. If the plan changes, you'll have a lot of magic to weave.'

Yesfir gave her father a stiff nod.

Emad had to bite his tongue while he listened to his brother's plan.

Her being half-djinn made Roshan the least vulnerable to the seal. Her job was to raise portals to Baka for the prisoners to escape through. And because it was dark now and difficult to view the encampment through a destination window, Navid would go along as a scout.

Given their circumstances, the plan was a good one. With just the three of them going, Behrouz, Roshan and Navid, there would be significant room for manoeuvre if Armaiti warned the high magus. Emad, however, wanted to protest, remind Fiqitush that Navid had just returned from Arshak and had needed Yesfir to rescue him. And as for Roshan, while the lass was determined to help, he wasn't sure that would be enough to make a difference.

'Emad.'

He looked up and caught Fiqitush staring at him.

'What?'

'Put out your hand,' Fiqitush said. 'No, your right hand—weren't you listening?'

He ignored the question and held out his hand.

Roshan reached across and touched his bracelet.

Emad felt as if he stood at *Apkallu*'s tiller, a tailwind blowing against his back.

His jaw slackened when he realised what Roshan had done.

'You're to leave for Baka immediately,' he heard his brother say.

Fiqitush's voice sounded as though it came from outside the room. He wanted to raise a portal to Arshak and single-handedly slaughter the entire encampment, its high magus included.

'Roshan and the others should be back by tomorrow morning,' his brother continued. 'I want you to prepare Baka for their return and organise the daevas into shifts. Baka must be habitable and defendable within two days.'

Two days?

Emad supposed he should thank his brother instead of complaining. What with organising the daevas into shifts and preparing them to meet an impossible deadline, there wouldn't be time to worry about the twins.

18

Armaiti floated above the group crammed together in Fiqitush's chamber. If she were corporeal, she'd smile at the king making plans while knowing a sabaoth was spying on them. Over the past week, she'd developed a grudging respect for the djinn's resilience.

Again, she missed having a mouth to smile with when Roshan insisted on raising portals and nothing more.

Good work, Manah, Armaiti thought. *It looks like you've thoroughly deceived the girl.*

She had heard enough.

Armaiti rose through the palace's ceiling, the cavern's sandy roof and then emerged into the air and a dusk sky. She turned her ethereal body towards Arshak.

It took a thought to propel herself into the encampment and the high magus's tent.

Sassan sat at his table, writing his daily report to the emperor, the tablet he wrote on due for dispatch at dawn. The plaque with its twenty satrapies leaned against a table leg, and the amphora of diluted poppy juice had yet to be returned to the apothecary.

She read his report and found no mention of the seal or the

mess he'd made trying to master it. He had highlighted he had Iram's location, its coordinates, and was searching for a way to get a daeva to raise a portal to the hidden city. While the irony of what he'd written was lost on Sassan—using the very magic he was punishing daevas for practising—his report gave her an idea.

Armaiti reached into his brain and took control of the areas responsible for writing. The hand holding the stylus stopped moving. She experienced Sassan's limbs shake. After she had calmed him, she began to write on the lower half of the tablet's wet clay. Fascinated and horrified in equal measure, Sassan focussed on his possessed hand rather than on what it wrote.

Armaiti severed the connection between themselves. She waited to check Sassan had read and understood her message. He read it silently the first time and then out loud the second time. On the first read, he'd found the last sentence ambiguous.

Tonight, the djinn will come to Arshak to rescue the daeva prisoners. Find the king of the djinn in Iram. Kill him and Iram will fall. Put yourself between the seal and the daeva who will deliver your men to Iram.

She remained until, after his fifth reading, Sassan understood what he had to do to raise a portal into Iram.

19

Zana saw a flesh tone above a circle of white, and beneath the circle lay shades of buff.

'Zana.'

Tired, stiff and thirsty, Zana ignored the voice that sounding like Nahrian's. It was a trick.

'The sun's setting, Zana. You passed the test.'

He raised his eyes and nothing else. His temples ached from the effort. The horizon had turned a golden brown.

Neck muscle by neck muscle, he raised his head. The aches turned sharper, causing his vision to blur with tears. The joints in his legs, shoulders and hips had tightened and refused to comply. He gritted his teeth, stood and, ignoring the shooting pains, stretched.

Dressed in a robe, Nahrian poured water into the bowl in front of him.

Zana nodded his appreciation and drank.

After he'd finished drinking, he looked behind him.

'Where's Vul?' he said, his voice croaking.

Nahrian poured him a second bowlful.

'He left soon after I arrived.'

Zana felt nothing. He was neither pleased with himself nor satisfied he'd proved Vul wrong.

After his second bowl of water, and with Nahrian's help, he made his shaky way to the stairs.

He had to concentrate as he negotiated the first dozen steps, Nahrian leading the way. As his body grew more limber, he found it easier to keep up with her. Unlike her brother, Nahrian was content to descend the stairs in silence.

At the base of the mountain and still inside the cave, Nahrian poured him a third bowl of water.

'There's no need to talk,' she said. 'After I completed the test, my throat was so dry, I couldn't speak until the next morning.'

Zana nodded his appreciation.

Although he had a sore throat, the reason for his reticence was his memory of the lioness. He wanted to ask Nahrian about the things Vul saw and how many of them proved wrong. Zana got the impression Nahrian knew little or nothing about his past life. He didn't want to tell her about an old lioness being abandoned by her cub. Even though he'd been four at the time, Zana found it hard to accept what he'd done. The last thing he wanted now was for Nahrian, who'd been kind to him, to judge him.

They stopped when they reached the city's entrance.

'I'll see you soon,' Nahrian said.

Zana cleared his throat.

'I look forward to it,' he said, then blushed because he'd meant it.

Inside Baka, the city was dark except for the buildings clustered around the only functioning well. Golden lamplight poured from open windows and also from the rooftops, where people dined, their conversations more curbed than lively.

Zana's dry throat wasn't the reason he headed for the city's wells.

Two of the city's three wells were dry. Boarding covered the third to prevent sand from getting into it. Exhausted and thirsty, Zana grabbed the edge of the wood with his teeth and pulled the cover far enough to one side to drop a bucket into the gap he'd made. The bucket presented more of a problem. Careful not to let it fall into the well until he had the rope attached to its handle between his teeth, Zana lifted the bucket onto the edge.

'Zana, wait.' The voice came from a woman sitting at a table on a rooftop. She stood. The two children sitting opposite her swung off their bench. A man got up and took their hands before they could get too close to the parapet. 'I'll be down in a moment,' she called.

Zana still held the rope between his teeth while he waited. How much trouble was he having that a daeva had to help him get a drink? And how did she know his name?

The daeva strode across the space between them. When she reached him, she held out her hand.

'Here, let me take that,' she said, and pointed at the rope.

Zana watched as she lowered the bucket into the well. She hadn't lowered it far when he heard its base slap the water.

'According to legend, this and the other two wells aren't really wells,' the daeva said, then hauled up the bucket. 'The water doesn't come from a water source beneath us. It's supplied by the remains of some ancient djinn magic.'

Unsure of what to say, Zana said, 'Thank you for your help.'

The daeva hefted the bucket onto the edge of the well and then lowered it to the ground for Zana to take a drink.

'Behrouz said that if ever you got separated, this is where you'd meet,' she said. 'He apologises for not waiting for you. He was called back to Iram. If you're hungry, you could join us. The children have been waiting since dusk to meet you.'

Zana glanced at the rooftop. The children, their faces hidden behind shadow and—from their heights—no more than seven years old, waved. Zana raised a paw and gave them his best smile.

He thanked the daeva again and then helped her drag the

boarding back into place. 'I've already eaten,' he lied. 'I'll just stay here and sleep while I wait for Father to come and get me.'

It was too dark to tell if he'd hurt the daeva's feelings, but after spending a whole afternoon without water and moving, he knew he wouldn't be the best company, especially around children.

The daeva nodded.

'Just call if you need anything,' she said. 'My husband will be up for another hour.'

Zana watched her leave. He looked up and gave the children another wave before settling down to wait.

He wondered how furious Father would be with him for disappearing. What was going on in Iram that he'd been called back? Or was his waiting here some kind of punishment?

Zana rested his chin on a front leg. He thought about the old lioness, his real mother, and her broken heart. Zana's eyes grew heavy. At the sound of footsteps, he opened his eyes wider.

A couple dressed in robes approached, the glow of a firestone in the shorter of the two's hand.

Zana's pulse quickened. He sat up.

'Nahrian,' he said, recognising the face illuminated by the firestone's beige glow. The taller woman had the same amber eyes and auburn hair as Nahrian's. The deep lines creasing her brow suggested she didn't smile much. She walked with her broad shoulders thrown back and looked straight ahead as though she feared nothing.

'Hello again,' Nahrian said. She gestured at the woman next to her. 'This is my mother, Ramina. She's the leader of the Cross Scar pride.'

Zana bowed, hiding his surprise.

'May we join you?' Ramina said. Her voice carried a lilt that put Zana at ease.

'Please,' he said, and shuffled back so mother and daughter could sit on the edge of the well.

'I heard you passed our test, Zana,' Ramina said, gathering

her robe around her. 'It was very hot on the mountain today.' Nahrian held the firestone, making it difficult for Zana to see her mother's face. 'Vul tells me you're serious about learning to shape-shift.'

Just how much does Vul know about me?

'I am,' he said to Ramina.

'I would be glad to teach you, if you were to ask me for help.'

Ramina tilted her head and nodded.

Zana's cheeks burned. A smile stretched his lips. Ramina continued, giving him no time to respond.

'There is, however, a condition—one I'm not sure you'll be happy to agree to. If I'm to teach you, you must become a member of my pride.'

A jolt ran through Zana's body and suppressed his breathless excitement.

'You want me to leave Mother, Father and the others?'

Ramina answered with a stern nod.

This was the reason Vul had said all those things to him.

'I'm sorry,' Zana said. He did his best to ignore Nahrian's frown. 'For now, until I know everyone is safe, I can't leave them to join you.'

Even in the thin glow of the firestone, Zana caught Ramina's smile.

Zana glanced across at Nahrian. He hadn't expected Ramina to react that way.

'Mother was testing you,' Nahrian said, looking pleased.

Another test?

'It was a test of your loyalty,' Ramina said. 'Loyalty to the pride is paramount, Zana. I understand why you must remain here. When you're ready, there will be a place for you among the Cross Scar pride.'

Ramina lowered the neckline of her robe, and Nahrian did the same. She raised her firestone so Zana could see the white cross-shaped scar on the right shoulder of both mother and daughter.

'When you're ready, just approach the northernmost mountain,' Ramina continued. 'I promise there'll be someone to receive you.' She stood. 'Until then, protect the pride, Zana.'

Zana rose onto all fours.

'Thank you, Ramina,' he said.

Nahrian looked pleased when she smiled.

'Will I see you tomorrow? I'm helping to dig out sand from the northern watchtower.'

He wasn't sure what he was doing tomorrow.

'I hope so,' he said.

Zana watched the manticores depart. Even though he smiled, he found his chest ached a little.

What would it be like to wear such a scar, to see it on the shoulders of other members, of the pride he belonged to?

He glanced up at the rooftop the family had occupied. A lone figure sat at the table and stared up at the stars. Zana had needed the daeva's wife to help him get a drink from the well. But he hadn't needed to shape-shift to protect Roshan in Derbicca.

Zana lay down. He rested his chin on a foreleg and closed his eyes.

You can still make a difference, he told himself.

20

Sassan stared at the tablet and the message he'd written beneath his report to the emperor. The wedge-like shapes matched those produced by his stylus, and the spacing between the words and the lines of text matched the report he'd been writing. God, however, had then conveyed His message through Sassan's hand.

The past seven days, everything—the visions, the signs, the sabaoth's arrow and the seal—had led up to this moment. Sassan put down the tablet. His hand shook. Across from the tablet lay the amphora and the golden arrow. He picked up the amphora. The weight of its contents and the coolness of its surface reassured him.

Put yourself between the seal's power and the daeva who will deliver your men to Iram.

He'd read that last part of the message several times before he'd gone to see General Afacan. Then, back in his tent, he'd read it again to be sure of his interpretation.

Even though his eyes were open, he still saw Pudil, the bulging veins on his neck and temples glowing as if fire and not blood flowed through them.

God sent the message, Sassan reminded himself. *If there's pain, it's because He's testing you. He wants to know if you're still worthy of His favour.*

Sassan put down the amphora. It would still be there after they'd raised the portal.

Sassan smoothed the creases from his tunic, picked up the sabaoth's arrow, then left the tent.

With a guardsman following behind, Sassan made his way to the back of the encampment and beyond it, to a place that no one could see from Arshak's ramparts.

He found General Afacan, the manacled daeva, Tamraz, and fifteen men—three magi and twelve guardsmen armed with swords, shields, bows and arrows—waiting for him.

The men, except for the daeva, stood to attention. The general approached. Sassan waited, but all he received from Afacan was a stiff nod.

Sassan filled the uncomfortable silence with 'Think, speak and act well, General.'

The general's reply sounded like a criticism. After the morning's failed experiment with Pudil, Sassan knew the general didn't approve of this endeavour.

'Are the men ready for the rescue attempt, General?'

'They are, High Magus.'

'And they know I want at least one djinni captured alive?'

'Yes, High Magus.'

The general sounded as brittle as his behaviour.

'Very well,' Sassan said, then stepped around him. He reached the guardsmen and magi. He raised his right hand. The fifteen knelt on one knee and received his blessing.

The men stood, and the general joined him.

'Are they familiar with the city's layout Tamraz provided?' Sassan said.

The general began with a curt nod. 'As well as they could be in the limited time we've had to prepare.'

Sassan heard the dissension, expected it.

'High Magus, are you certain you can return the men to Arshak?'

Sassan glowered at the general.

'General Afacan, if I'm able to raise a portal into Iram, *then* I will raise a portal to transport them back. As we've already discussed, I and Tamraz will arrive outside Iram at dawn, and we will wait for them.'

The general glanced at the daeva with what Sassan took for pity.

He won't suffer the same fate as Pudil, Sassan thought. *I'll prove you and the others wrong.*

Sassan had spent his life proving others wrong.

He waved for Tamraz to approach.

'Unshackle him, General,' he said.

Sassan expected the general to huff at being tasked with something he'd order one of his own men to do. The general stepped forward and removed the pins from the manacles around the daeva's wrists and ankles. Afacan then gave the daeva a nod and wished him good luck.

Sassan used his mounting fury to calm his fear. Even though it was late at night, he sweated beneath his tunic. Sassan squeezed the sabaoth's arrow and held his breath.

The neckline and underarms of Tamraz's tunic, he noticed, had darkened, too.

He'd found the daeva that afternoon. Unlike the others, Tamraz hadn't tried to flee Arshak. His willingness to convert, so he and his wife could return to their home above his cobbler's workshop, had made him compliant. Sassan had made light use of the seal to compel him. And the information he'd volunteered, that King Fiqitush's magic held up the cavern Iram hid in, confirmed what his possessed hand had written: *Find the king of the djinn in Iram. Kill him and Iram will fall.*

'May I join your aura to mine, High Magus?' Tamraz said.

This is God's will, Sassan told himself. His bowels felt as if they were about to rebel.

'Go ahead, Tamraz,' he said, then braced himself.

The pain he'd expected didn't come. Sassan watched the daeva raise a destination window. Through it he saw a city swathed mostly in darkness. To his left he saw the outlines of buildings illuminated by light escaping from the windows of those surrounding them. Above the city, stars shone, which made little sense to Sassan. Iram, Tamraz had told him, was a city hidden underground. In the distance, something round gleamed. Sassan squinted and made out a golden dome illuminated by firestones arranged around its circumference at random intervals.

Tamraz wove the boarding window, then fused the second window to the first to form a portal with a brown edge. That was when Sassan's skin glowed and he felt as if every particle of himself had combusted.

Instinct told him to take off the seal, cut off the supply of djinn auric energy flowing through his body and into his aura.

His hand wouldn't move. His mouth wouldn't move either. All he could do was watch as the first of the fifteen men marched through the portal.

He fought to remain lucid as his insides boiled. He screamed to himself, *God is testing me. God is testing me.*

Heat rose from within him. His vision wavered and then blurred while the incursion into Iram continued.

Sassan felt certain he no longer breathed, that liquid bubbled and sloshed inside his chest.

My lungs have liquified.

As if to confirm the thought, vertical streams of bubbles, no bigger than pinpricks, filled his vision. The occasional flash of brown from Tamraz's portal hit the back of his eyes.

His final thought was that, like his lungs, the insides of his eyeballs boiled.

A colourless, soundless and odourless void surrounded him.

A hand shook him. Sassan opened his eyes.

'Huh? What?'

Tamraz and General Afacan stood before him, both of them frowning. Sassan recognised fear on the daeva's face and concern on the general's. Beyond them lay empty ground: no guardsmen and magi, no portal.

Sassan's mouth and throat were parched. Otherwise, he might have cried out with relief.

'Are you all right, High Magus?' the general said.

Sassan nodded.

Tears filled his eyes. The pain of moving his head reminded him of the time his horse had bolted and he'd cricked his neck. Sassan cleared his throat.

'I'll return here at dawn to collect your men and my magi, General.' Sassan's voice sounded strangled. He turned his whole body so he could face the daeva. 'Thank you, Tamraz.'

The walk back to his tent was slow and agony-filled. Unable to control his muscles and endure the pain, he voided his bladder before he was halfway to his tent. Sassan hoped the darkness and limited torchlight hid the mishap, but he was in too much pain to care as he struggled to remain conscious.

Sassan ignored the guards' salute and stumbled into his tent. He'd forgotten he still held the sabaoth's arrow until he tried to uncork the amphora. The arrow dropped onto the table with a *clang*. Sassan's hands shook so much, he used his teeth to rip out the cork.

From somewhere inside of him a voice issued a warning. If he were to keep his promise to the general, he'd have to be up in eight hours. The thought of Tamraz raising another two portals —one to Iram to collect the guardsmen and magi, and then another to return them to Arshak—made him bilious. He'd have to endure his insides liquifying another *two times*.

Sassan ignored the warning and emptied the rest of the amphora's contents into his mouth.

21

While Yesfir and Behrouz argued, Roshan tried to look anywhere but at them. She, together with the king and the prince, stood at the other end of the audience chamber to give the couple some space.

Behrouz's suggestion of not wearing his bracelet to avoid the seal's influence had seemed like a good idea. But then the prince had said the rescue would take twice as long. Without his bracelet, Behrouz's auric energy would quickly run out, forcing them to stick together and leaving Roshan the only one able to raise portals to Baka. Yesfir had argued that she should be the one to go with Roshan, because she stood a better chance of resisting the seal. When Solomon had used it on both of them, Behrouz had surrendered more of his auric energy than Yesfir.

'They're taking too long,' the king said.

Prince Emad's eyes widened.

'I'll go.'

The king's attention flitted between Roshan and his brother.

'Whoever goes with Roshan has to wear their bracelet,' the king said.

Roshan saw both brothers exchange a look.

'Do you think those two can hear each other's thoughts, like we can?'

Navid's head poked out of Roshan's open satchel. She reached into it and pulled him out.

'If they could, it might explain why the prince has been behaving so strangely.'

'You're needed in Baka,' the king said.

The prince shook his head.

'You're sending both of them, Fiqitush. Why not others?'

The king straightened and folded his arms.

'Not now, *Emad*. This isn't the time to question my decision.'

The prince rested his hands on his hips.

'Before they leave is the perfect time.'

The king shook his head and unfolded his arms.

'How else would they learn what they're capable of? I know how valuable they are to the djinn and daevas, but I won't lock them away for safekeeping. Everyone's busy with the evacuation. We need all the help we can get.'

Navid twisted in Roshan's hand as he tried to reach her forearm. He didn't want to go back into her satchel.

'Who are they talking about?' he said. 'Behrouz and Yesfir or us?'

Roshan remembered her last visit to the king and how the prince wanted to send her and Navid off to some faraway place by ship.

'The prince has behaved like this before, though I don't know why.'

'Ask him.' Her brother sounded uncharacteristically angry. 'We're about to head into a camp filled with three thousand guardsmen, and everyone around us is arguing.'

Nine hours earlier, an arrow had wounded Navid. It might have killed him, if Yesfir hadn't rescued him. No wonder he was anxious.

'Excuse me,' she said. 'Who are you taking about? My brother and me'—she tilted her head at Behrouz and Yesfir—'or them?'

The king glowered at the prince.

'Tell them,' the king said.

The prince's expression, first incredulous, turned furious. Prince Emad shook his head vigorously, and Roshan thought he might hit the king.

'All right, it's decided,' Behrouz called. 'Roshan, let's go.'

She felt her brother's interest piqued, and so was her own. The king and the prince were hiding something.

'Tell us what?' Roshan said.

The prince stepped forward and away from his brother. He led her towards Yesfir and Behrouz.

'We'll talk when you both get back,' he said. As if he shouldn't have touched her, he pulled his hand away. 'Concentrate on your mission and come back safely. No heroics—got that?'

Back in Derbicca, when he'd insisted she and Yesfir return to Iram, he'd looked ready to murder her. What had changed? And why did he seem unsure of himself and uncomfortable around her?

'Forget about it for now,' Navid said. 'He's right: we need to concentrate on the mission.' As they drew closer to the husband and wife, Navid sighed his relief. 'It looks like Behrouz made the right decision.'

The former daeva's eyes blazed red.

'He's wearing his bracelet,' Roshan said, sharing her brother's relief.

All she trusted herself to do was release the prisoners and herd them through a portal into Baka. If Behrouz had decided not to wear his bracelet and they ran into trouble, she'd have more than raising portals to keep her busy. Roshan wasn't sure if she could curb her thoughts in a crisis.

Before she could raise a portal, Yesfir hugged her and kissed her cheek. She kissed her fingertip and touched Navid between his ears.

'Please be careful,' she said. 'If there's any sign of trouble, raise a portal and get out of there.' She glared at Behrouz. 'And that means you, too.'

Behrouz straightened his sword belt and then gave Yesfir a hug.

'Both of you do as she says,' the king said. 'And Emad's right: no heroics. Am I understood?'

Behrouz bowed and Roshan nodded.

Yesfir raised the portal. Roshan saw the prince wave, his face pale. Behrouz stepped through first.

Roshan emerged behind a tall, rocky outcrop. Behrouz raised a dome of invisibility and silence large enough to accommodate them both.

The encampment appeared brighter than she remembered. She'd last viewed it through a destination window an hour before. At this time of night, surely, someone would have given the order to extinguish some torches, not to light more of them. She shared her concern with Behrouz.

'You're right,' he said. 'It seems brighter. Perhaps Armaiti warned the high magus.'

The daevas' capture had been her fault. They had to continue with the rescue.

Her brother heard the thought.

'If it's impossible to mount a rescue,' Navid said, 'we shouldn't stay.'

She agreed, and then said to Behrouz, 'If they're expecting us, be ready to raise a portal and leave.'

Behrouz beamed her a reassuring smile.

'I will.' He placed a hand on her shoulder. 'If you're uncertain about anything, return to Iram. If anything were to happen to you'—he pointed at his eyes and the flames surrounding his irises—'others won't get the second chance I've had.'

She remembered the king's words to his brother.

I know how valuable they are to the djinn and daevas, but I won't lock them away for safekeeping.

She bent her head back to meet Behrouz's gaze.

'We have to try. I owe it to those daevas to at least find out if there's a chance of freeing them.'

Behrouz nodded.

'Let's go.'

Roshan took two steps for every one of Behrouz's. Halfway to the camp, she lifted Navid out of her satchel and let him climb onto her shoulder. They drew closer and Roshan's certainty increased: they were expected. More torches had been lit, but those on guard duty hadn't doubled or tripled. Could the trap set for them be waiting in or among the cluster of tents the prisoners were being kept in?

'I'll take a look before you get too close,' Navid said.

They skirted around the edge of the camp and saw a narrow corridor. It led to an open area and the cluster of five tents in which the daevas were being held. Roshan put out a hand to stop Behrouz from entering the corridor.

'Navid will scout ahead,' she said. Though they were inside a dome of invisibility and silence, she kept her voice low. She led Behrouz over to a shadowed area, lifted Navid from her shoulder and placed him on the sand.

Roshan swallowed.

'Be careful,' she said.

Her brother scurried away and along the edge of a tent. The space between Roshan's shoulders tightened.

Behrouz sat down. He patted the ground next to him.

'Standing is tiring and only frays my nerves.'

She couldn't imagine Behrouz getting nervous about anything. Roshan sat down among the shadows and waited.

A pair of soldiers on guard duty passed them twice before she spotted movement from her right. Navid darted down the lit corridor between two tents. Anyone passing would have seen him. Roshan held her breath. She released it only when no one had raised the alarm.

Navid stopped in front of them. He sniffed the air. Roshan had to remind herself they were invisible. She pushed her cupped hand through the dome. Navid backed away before jumping into it.

No sooner was he in the dome than she experienced his distress.

'Only two of the five tents are occupied,' he said, and described their positions relative to the other three. 'They're mostly filled with the older daevas. I only saw one child. There are four daevas in one tent and five in the other.'

She repeated his message to Behrouz, and then said, 'What do we do?'

Behrouz rubbed the back of his neck.

'If the high magus is using the seal, he'll want to coerce those who can maintain spells for longer than the older daevas. He's filled those two tents with daevas he doesn't want.'

After hearing about the tent catching fire and the high magus threatening the son of the daeva he interrogated, Behrouz's conclusion didn't surprise Roshan.

'Do you think they'll spring a trap while we rescue them?' she said.

Behrouz ran his fingers through the sand, his brow creased.

'No,' he said. 'They'll raise our confidence by letting us rescue those daevas first. Then we'll go searching for the others. That's when they'll pounce.'

'I'll go see if there are other daevas beyond those tents,' Navid said.

Roshan passed on what Navid planned on doing. She spoke aloud to her brother.

'Are you sure? If they're expecting us, they'll most likely be expecting one of us to be a rat.'

She felt her brother stiffen and knew he'd recalled events from earlier in the day.

'Even with the torches, there are plenty of shadows for me to hide in,' he said. 'Like you, I think we should at least find out if it's possible to rescue the others.'

Behrouz listened as Roshan repeated her brother's answer.

'All right,' he said. 'For a rat, the encampment is a huge place with a lot of tents to search.' He pointed at the stars to gauge the time. 'You have an hour, Navid. Your sister and I will return here after we've freed those daevas. If any of us has a problem, we retreat to the rock we arrived behind. If the situation gets bad, we return to Iram.' One side of his mouth curved down. 'Navid, if there's trouble and we're not here, get to that rock and wait there. One of us will come back for you.'

Behrouz's words troubled her. They were expecting Navid to put himself in the same danger he'd faced earlier. Back then, the high magus wasn't expecting anyone.

Her brother jumped from her hand.

'Stop worrying,' he said. 'And can we please get on with it? The longer we stay here and talk, the more likely I'll change my mind.' He ran through the dome and disappeared into the shadows.

Behrouz took Navid's abrupt departure as his cue to stand. He held out a hand and pulled Roshan up.

'Raise yourself a dome of invisibility,' he said, 'and make sure it won't absorb light and cast shadows. You take the nearest tent, the one with the four daevas inside it. I'll go first.'

Her throat had dried, so she nodded. She wasn't sure who she was more afraid for: her brother or herself.

Roshan raised a dome. She felt it being tugged as Behrouz stepped away from her and disappeared. A count to thirty followed before she made her way down the corridor of tents.

After sitting within the shadowed edge of the encampment, the torchlight hurt her eyes. The farther in she went, the brighter the torchlight and the warmer it grew. Every ten steps, she checked the intense light hadn't penetrated her dome and cast her shadow.

The lack of guardsmen guarding the five tents made her chew her lower lip. Roshan entered the tent closest to her. Like Navid had said, the silhouettes of four daevas lay inside it. Roshan extended her dome of invisibility to encompass the prisoners. She pulled a firestone from her pocket. Still clutching the firestone, she tugged her tunic's sleeve until it was halfway down her forearm. She activated the firestone. Three of the four daevas squinted. Roshan held a finger to her lips and raised her forearm so they could see her bracelet.

On one side of the tent, a woman cradled a boy no older than five. A middle-aged male lay on the other, sweating and shivering. Next to him, a white-haired man leaned over and dabbed at the sheen on the younger daeva's forehead.

Roshan raised a portal and gestured at the woman and child to enter.

'My husband, they separated us,' she said, her eyes bloodshot.

Roshan tried to sound more confident than she felt.

'We'll find him,' she said, and then waved her through the portal. Next, she turned her attention to the two male daevas. 'What's wrong with him?'

The older daeva shrugged.

'The high magus has Solomon's seal,' he said. 'I never thought I'd set eyes on that evil thing again. The high magus isn't like Solomon: he doesn't know how to use it. He's been testing it on us.' He pointed at the prone daeva. 'He used it on Basi, here, and tried to get him to raise a portal to Iram. Basi wouldn't—he resisted the seal—but it left him like this.'

Not sure what else she could do for Basi, she touched his bracelet. The shivering stopped, and the daeva's breathing became deeper and steadier.

'What did you do to Basi?' the daeva said. He bent forward and smiled. 'How did you do that?'

Roshan ignored him and uttered a levitation incantation. Basi rose into the air and then through the portal.

'Go,' she said to the daeva. 'They'll take care of you in Baka.'

The daeva stepped towards the portal and stopped.

'You're not a djinni and you're not a daeva—are you?' he said.

Unsure what she was, she shook her head.

Roshan watched him leave and then collapsed the portal.

She shrank her dome of invisibility and exited the tent. Roshan used the breathing exercises Yesfir had taught her and focussed on exiting the encampment without being detected.

Back and sitting on the edge of the encampment, surrounded by her dome and shadows, Roshan wondered how she could put a stop to Sassan and this madness.

She closed her eyes to calm herself. Roshan saw a pile of charcoal. She remembered the exercise Manah had set her and how she'd failed at preventing an individual piece from scorching the others. Roshan opened her eyes.

One of them had to return to Iram and warn the king an invasion could be sooner than later.

Behrouz would be back soon. Not finding her here would worry him. Best she waited—but not for too long.

22

Emad entered the audience chamber to find Fiqitush and Yesfir seated in front of a destination window pointed at the encampment outside Arshak. The thought of Roshan and Navid wandering around a camp filled with three thousand soldiers and only Behrouz to protect them made him sweat.

As he drew closer, he saw them viewing what looked to be a well-lit part of the camp. Towards the edge of the destination window, the other areas of the encampment weren't so well lit.

'How's it going?' he asked.

Fiqitush looked over his shoulder.

'They've sent nine of the prisoners through to Baka.' His brow creased. 'Isn't that where you're supposed to be?'

Emad had spent the past three hours developing a plan and accompanying work rotas for Baka's restoration. Now, however, didn't seem a good time to say so. With over thirty daevas held captive, what about the others they were supposed to have rescued? Emad saw how Yesfir hadn't moved since his arrival, her attention fixed on the centre of the destination window.

'Is there a problem?' Emad said.

'Your Majesty, Your Majesty.'

The call came from the hallway outside. Sandals slapped against tiles. Whoever it was, he ran towards the chamber.

Shephatiah burst in.

'Your Majesty,' he said, then took a deep breath to control his panting. 'Empire soldiers are in Iram.'

As if one, Yesfir and Fiqitush rose. Yesfir clung to her father's shoulder.

'How many?' Emad said.

Shephatiah resembled a child about to be told off.

'I don't know,' he said. 'They set off several of the pavement alarms in the city's unoccupied half. When those on watch reached the triggered alarms, they saw a magus raise a dome of invisibility over a group of armed soldiers. There wasn't time to count them.'

Fiqitush pursed his lips, his eyes fixed on the dais at the front of the chamber. The muscles around Emad's stomach tightened. His brother, however, looked as if an incursion were an everyday occurrence.

He patted his daughter's hand.

'Yesfir,' he said, 'I need you to keep an eye on your husband and the twins. I'll leave someone behind to guard you. If you encounter any problems, raise a portal to Baka. Understand?'

Yesfir's hand slipped from his shoulder.

'Should we abort the mission?' she said.

Fiqitush shook his head.

'The high magus tortured a daeva to get the coordinates for Iram. I don't want to think about what he's done to raise a portal here. Those daevas are our people—we have to rescue them. And we need to save them before the high magus finds more ways to use our people against us.'

Yesfir kissed her father's cheek. She sat down and continued her vigil in front of the destination window.

Fiqitush raised a portal.

'Emad, Shephatiah, come with me.'

The portal opened inside the second tier of the ziggurat in the unoccupied half of the city. Two other djinn had arrived earlier. They both acknowledged the king with a nod.

The tier and the windows in all four of its walls gave Emad a sweeping view of the city below. Like the others, he kept his distance from the arched windows to avoid being caught by the moonlight streaming through the cavern's ceiling.

Thanks to the magus's dome of invisibility, the city below appeared uninhabited. There was no telling how many soldiers and magi had sneaked into Iram.

'Can you see anything?' Fiqitush whispered.

Emad shook his head.

'We need to expose them,' Emad replied. 'Until we know how many there are, we don't know what we're dealing with.'

Fiqitush waved over Shephatiah.

'I want all the children moved to the ziggurat opposite this one,' he said. 'Keep everyone under domes of invisibility and silence. If there's any sign of trouble, if it looks as if other soldiers might storm the occupied half, stop work on packing the library's tablets and papyri. I want all the remaining djinn to leave for Baka.' He checked Shephatiah understood, and then said, 'Go.'

Emad understood his brother's prudence. But it didn't help them with figuring out what they were dealing with and whether to either defend the city long enough to move what remained of the djinn's history to Baka or evacuate Iram. He stared up at the moonlight filtering through the sand above them. The silvery light gave the djinn an advantage, if they could—

'I've got an idea,' Emad said. He pulled his brother closer and pointed at the cavern's ceiling. 'The sand, the fine stuff, we make some of it—a small amount—fall onto both halves of the city.'

Fiqitush raised an eyebrow and chewed his lower lip.

'We could,' he said. His eyes brightened as Emad's idea took shape. 'Are you thinking the sand sticks to the dome, or they leave behind a trail of footsteps?'

Emad shrugged.

'Any or all,' he said. 'We can't just sit here and watch. We have to do something.'

Fiqitush approached a window and muttered an incantation. A silver cloud of sand particles wafted down towards the city.

'San, Toma,' Fiqitush said, addressing the two djinn still on the second tier, 'send word to the lookouts on both sides of the city and let them know what we're doing.'

The djinn raised portals and disappeared into them.

'Apart from the alarms and the lookouts,' Emad said, 'what else have you prepared for our unwanted visitors?'

Fiqitush groaned.

'Nothing,' he said. 'There hasn't been time. I assumed the high magus would try to snatch a djinni, but I never imagined he'd try so soon.'

Emad cringed. He hadn't meant to discourage his brother.

'If anyone can handle this, it's you,' he said.

Emad felt his bracelet pulse. His brother touched his own and must have received the same alert. Emad raised a dome of invisibility and silence around the two of them and signalled for his brother to follow him. A thought had accompanied the pulse. Rather than words, the thought contained a compulsion. Standing before the window facing the waterfall at the back of the cavern, both brothers looked to their right and in the palace's direction.

The fine sand stuck to a single dome's surface glistened in the moonlight. One moment spherical and the next oval, the dome accommodated the width of the streets it passed through.

'They're heading for the palace,' Fiqitush said. 'And from its size, I doubt there's more than a dozen men beneath that dome.'

The muscles around Emad's stomach uncoiled a little. This wasn't an invasion. But then he shook his head.

They're here for the king. What good would killing him do? The djinn wouldn't just disappear because they killed Fiqitush.

'But Iram would.'

'What was that?' Fiqitush said.

Unsure of how his brother would react, Emad spoke plainly.

'Those soldiers aren't just here for a djinni. The high magus sent them here to kill you. I don't know how, but he knows that if you die, Iram dies with you.'

His brother's calmness only added to Emad's distress.

'Then we evacuate Iram,' Fiqitush said. 'Let the soldiers find the city empty.'

Emad glanced to his left.

'Yesfir's still inside the palace,' he said. 'We need to get her out of there.'

Fiqitush nodded. He held his hands behind his back as if he were about to take a stroll.

'Go get her and leave.'

About to raise a portal, Emad hesitated.

'If everyone leaves, you're coming too—aren't you?'

Fiqitush frowned.

'I told you before, Iram and I are bound. I can't leave.'

Emad shook his head. So, Fiqitush and the city were bound. That didn't mean his brother couldn't leave. If the djinn and their king relocated, Iram collapsing in Fiqitush's absence wasn't a problem.

Emad felt his bracelet pulse again. This time, the message, the sensation it conveyed, was for them to look down the main road and away from the palace.

Together they turned.

Halfway up the main road, a single figure marched towards the palace. Humanoid, its surface, however, matched the colour of the surrounding rock and stone brickwork.

Emad's legs trembled. He'd only ever heard of them and had never seen one. The magic used to animate them had belonged to the nation Solomon had ruled. No one knew how the empire had obtained such magic, but the figure heading towards the palace was proof it had. At the other end of the road, behind the golem, Emad guessed there had to be at least two magi who'd constructed the creature from the surrounding rock and controlled it.

He saw how Fiqitush had already raised a portal, the palace reflected in its destination window.

'What are you doing?' Emad said. 'Are you mad, Fiqitush?'

Instead of answering, his brother pointed at the portal with his chin and then stepped through it. Emad joined him.

With both of them standing in front of the palace, Fiqitush collapsed the portal. He began an incantation Emad recognised.

He's erecting a dome of protection around the palace.

'We need to collect Yesfir and leave, Fiqitush.'

His brother wasn't listening. His gaze kept wandering between the dust-coated dome of invisibility and the golem marching towards them.

Emad's voice quavered. 'Fiqitush, please don't do anything stupid.'

His brother faced him and smiled.

'If they kill me here,' he pointed at the cavern's roof, 'they'll bring down Iram.' His smile lacked any humour.

Emad felt sick.

Fiqitush closed his eyes and touched his bracelet.

He's telling everyone to get ready to leave.

'I'll draw the soldiers towards me,' Fiqitush said. 'Get Yesfir. I'll drop the dome and let you through.'

If Fiqitush thought he could hand the mantle to him and give up, he was wrong. Emad pursed his lips.

'I lost Aeshma three days ago. I won't let you sacrifice yourself like this. There has to be another way.'

His brother eyed the dome and then the approaching golem.

'There isn't time for a debate. If you've a plan that avoids us both getting killed, I'm all ears. Otherwise, go get Yesfir and leave.'

The rush of the waterfall made it hard to think.

Emad rolled his eyes and groaned. The answer was right behind them.

'Get everyone onto a rooftop—the higher the better,' Emad said. 'We're going to divert water into the unoccupied half of Iram.'

23

Navid guessed he'd been travelling east for the past half hour, following the northern edge of the encampment. He'd found nothing, not even a clue to suggest where they'd hidden the daevas. Compared to the area in which he'd found the five tents, this part of the camp was poorly lit.

Navid stopped to think.

They had walked into a trap. He, Roshan and Behrouz had agreed on that much. Whoever had set the lure would want to make it easy for them to find the other prisoners.

Navid turned right and headed deeper into the encampment, keeping to the edges of tents and avoiding exposed areas of sand. Every twenty paces, he stopped, looked up to see if he could locate a section of the camp filled with more torches than others. After several stops, he spotted a shaft of golden light that cut through the darkness. Navid took another right turn.

Farther up, he slowed and then stopped when he saw a movement in the shadows cast by a tent. As he edged closer, Navid's heartbeat quickened. So intent on the tent and whatever lay hiding within its shadow, Navid missed colliding with the sole of a boot. With caution, he backed away.

Pairs of guardsmen hid behind tents lining a space cleared of others except for two. Navid smelled the iron they carried, but it was too dark to tell whether they carried weapons, manacles or both.

Navid moved closer and between the tents, freezing whenever anyone looked his way. His heart beat so fast, it felt as if it thrummed inside his chest. More torches burned the closer he got. The light banished shadows and made it impossible to approach the pair of tents without being seen.

He kept close to the ground and sniffed the air, hoping to detect a faint odour coming from inside them. The smoke from the torches masked everything.

Navid doubled back. Once he'd cleared the tents and the hidden guardsmen, he took a sharp left and made his careful way back to the encampment's perimeter. On reaching its edge, he turned left again and kept to the shadows as he made his way over to the spot where Roshan and Behrouz agreed to wait for him.

There was no way the tents being watched could contain all the remaining prisoners. With seven daevas might crammed into each tent, the rest had to be hidden somewhere else in the camp, somewhere not so well lit.

Regardless of the guardsmen lying in wait, he knew his sister would want to attempt a rescue. As a novice, she'd always volunteered and tried to be helpful. Now was no exception, especially with Roshan believing the daevas' capture was her fault. She'd want to attempt a rescue, and even if they were successful, how would she react when she discovered she hadn't transported all the daevas to Baka?

They'd taken enough risks. If he had to, he'd change back into a human and carry his kicking and screaming sister through a portal and into Iram.

24

Roshan sensed her brother's apprehension before she saw him. She pushed her hand through her dome of invisibility and silence to let him know where she was.

'We were right,' he said, after describing what he'd found. 'They're expecting us and it's a trap. Unless you can come up with a way that won't get us captured, I'm afraid we're done here.'

Behrouz arrived and collapsed his dome. Roshan tapped Behrouz's booted foot and expanded her dome to accommodate the two of them.

'I sent just five old daevas to Baka,' Behrouz said.

Roshan described what Navid had told her, then added her own news.

'The high magus has Iram's coordinates,' she said. 'He's trying to raise portals to it. An invasion is happening sooner than later.'

Behrouz rubbed the back of his neck. He gazed at Roshan as if he were sorry for something.

'We have to return to Iram.'

Roshan wanted to scream at herself. All it took was a thought to deliver every daeva in this camp to Baka. But she still couldn't frame one in the unambiguous way Manah had taught her. Until she mastered that, she'd be a danger to others. For now, all she could do was remain committed and determined about helping the captured daevas.

'You go back and warn them,' she said to Behrouz. 'I can't leave those daevas behind.'

Navid squeaked.

'Is this about Daniyel?' her brother said. 'It's too dangerous for you to go in there alone. Besides, we don't know where the rest of the daevas are.'

Behrouz shook his head.

'Yesfir would kill me if I left you here. I know your mind's set on helping the daevas, and I want to too. But we must warn Iram first.'

Lightness filled Roshan's chest.

'You mean you'll help me?'

Behrouz stood and raised his hands, ready to weave a portal.

'But only after I've warned the king,' he said. 'Wait here. I won't be long.'

A destination window appeared in front of Behrouz, the image at its centre a blur of mauve.

'What's going on?' Navid said. 'What's wrong with his window?'

Behrouz muttered an incantation. He nudged the window's rim. The mauve blur persisted. He collapsed the window, touched his bracelet.

'She's safe,' he muttered to himself with a nod.

Roshan's anxiousness matched her brother's.

'What is it, Behrouz? You look worried.'

He rubbed the back of neck again.

'Iram's already being invaded,' he said. 'It's impossible to penetrate a dome of protection with a portal, and the palace is surrounded by one.'

Behrouz raised another destination window.

Roshan gazed into it. The king and his brother stood to one side of a mauve dome capping the palace. She touched her bracelet.

'He's telling the djinn to evacuate Iram,' she said. 'How can we can help?'

Behrouz shook his head.

'Yesfir's still watching us. While we can't enter the palace, she can leave the dome of protection whenever she wants to. If we're to rescue those daevas, we must do it now.'

Roshan picked up Navid. With Baka being evacuated, the only difference she could make was to the daevas being held in those two tents. She tried not to think about the ones hidden elsewhere in the encampment.

'I'll show you where the tents are,' Navid said.

She accessed his memory of the open area of sand and the tents within it. Roshan wove a destination window. Behrouz stepped closer for a better look.

Pairs of guardsmen, their swords unsheathed, knelt or squatted behind a half-dozen tents. With no signs of magi to sense the window, Roshan moved it forward, past the waiting guardsmen and into one of the two tents they watched.

The bright torchlight from outside lit the tent's interior, revealing seven manacled male daevas. Five slept and two were awake, sitting as if they were waiting for something—or someone.

They found the second tent no different: seven male daevas, younger than those they'd already rescued, manacled, and one of them awake.

'Now I know their location,' Roshan said, 'I can raise a portal into each tent and then a dome of invisibility and silence inside it. The guardsmen outside won't see my portal to Baka.'

Behrouz pointed at the wakeful daeva.

'That one,' he said. 'I'd wager he cries out the instant you arrive.'

She wanted to ask why he would do such a thing. And then Roshan remembered the high magus had Solomon's seal. He might have used it to compel the daeva into doing such a thing.

'I'll come with you,' Behrouz continued. 'You raise the portal to Baka, and I'll raise a dome of invisibility and silence.'

Navid squirmed in her hand.

'The daeva might cry out before Behrouz has raised his dome,' her brother said. 'Can he raise a dome from here?'

She shared Navid's idea with Behrouz.

Behrouz stared at the sand. He shook his head.

'It's a good idea, Navid, but risky. Without first being inside, it'll be difficult to raise a dome the right size. Too big and some or all of the tent will disappear. Too small and the dome might not cover one or more of the daevas. If we're unlucky, one of them might cry out.'

Navid rested in the crook of her arm. He sat on his hind legs and said, 'Use a sleep incantation to make sure they're all asleep.'

Navid's idea made Roshan smile.

'Navid mentioned using a sleep incantation.' She took up a position in front of the window and pointed at the watchful daeva. 'Let's see if it works.'

Djinn and human magic lost their potency over distance. With the prisoners nearby, it was worth a try.

Roshan stared at the daeva as she recited the incantation.

The daeva closed and then opened his eyes.

Roshan repeated the incantation.

The daeva opened his mouth and yawned.

'It's working,' Navid said.

She repeated the incantation a third time. The daeva's eyes grew heavy, drooped and closed.

She faced Behrouz. Although his face was grim, he nodded his approval.

'Looks like we have a plan,' he said. 'As soon as those daevas are safe, you and Navid go to Baka.'

Concern lined Behrouz's face. He'd put her needs before Yesfir's safety.

'We will, Behrouz,' she said, and nodded. 'Thank you.'

25

Emad drew his brother's attention to the waterfall.

'Place a destination window close to the soldiers and their dome of invisibility,' he told Fiqitush. 'I'll send the water through the boarding window. If we can injure the magus, the dome will collapse, and then we'll see what we're dealing with.'

Emad summoned Core power and began his incantation, but he held off the final words until his brother had woven and fused the windows. While he waited, Emad glanced over at the main road.

The golem had closed the distance between it and the palace at a pace that made Emad wipe sweat from his brow. A dot of emerald burned from the centre of its chest—the symbol of power a magus had drawn onto it. The symbol linked the golem to the magi who drew Core power to animate it and provide it with sufficient intelligence to complete its task.

Emad turned back to his brother. He still hadn't raised a destination window.

'What's taking so long?'

Fiqitush shook his head.

'I don't know. Every time I try to weave the window, it fades. There's something pushing against it.'

Emad saw sweat on his brother's brow. Fiqitush stiffened when he tried to weave another window.

'It could be their dome,' Emad said. 'Maybe it's protective and invisible. Weave a window farther back from it and closer to us. I'll increase the water flow to cover the added distance.'

The next destination window held. Fiqitush's grin reminded him of Aeshma's snarl. Emad made a slight adjustment to the incantation and then recited its final words.

He looked up and over at the top of the waterfall. Water coiled on itself to form a vortex, the end of which disappeared into the portal beneath it. Emad heard the gush before he had time to turn.

A jet of water collided with the dome, sending plumes upwards and sideways.

'It's not working,' Fiqitush said.

Emad added an amendment to the incantation. Behind him the twist of water constricted.

The jet struck the dome so hard, it bubbled and frothed, spume rising into the air and sliding down its sides.

'The magus inside should be feeling it now,' Emad said, and hoped he was right.

Dents pockmarked the dome's surface.

'It's working,' Fiqitush said, and grinned.

One moment the dome was there, the next a cluster of soldiers collapsed into a heap. The water sent most of them rolling backwards and deeper into the unoccupied half of the city.

Emad uttered the three words to end the incantation and cut off the water. The portal beneath the waterfall collapsed with a *snap*.

To their credit, and except for one fallen comrade, the dripping soldiers regrouped. Each soldier carried a round shield the size of a man's torso and strapped to their forearm. Emad counted eleven soldiers, excluding the one who still hadn't moved. A soldier carried someone draped over his shoulder as if they were a waterskin. Unlike the soldiers dressed in black, the unconscious waterskin wore all white.

'That's the magus,' Emad said. 'He won't be causing us any more trouble.'

Arrows rained upon the intruders. The soldiers put their shields to good use and only one of them went down. Emad's legs trembled at the ringing sound of the arrowheads striking the shields. Their dark grey colour confirmed his suspicion.

'Those shields aren't wooden, and they don't look like bronze,' he said.

The soldiers had formed a tight circle, their shields covering the immediate space above them and along their sides.

If he weren't scared, what looked like a giant metal beetle lurching towards them would have impressed him.

Fiqitush recited a wind incantation.

The air wailed and shook against the soldiers, flinging clouds of water droplets into the air.

'It's having no effect on them,' his brother said. He lowered his arms, and the wind died. The soldiers pressed on, water rippling beneath their feet. 'You're right; they're carrying iron shields. They're repelling our magic.'

A djinni stepped through a portal and to the side of the shields that formed an iron dome of protection. He tried to approach, his scimitar aflame. The iron repelled him and the djinni had to raise another portal to withdraw.

Emad shifted his attention to the approaching golem. The burning symbol on its chest wasn't clear yet, but it was close enough now for Emad to see how its wide neck tapered into a wedge instead of a head.

It's a battering ram with arms and legs.

'I have to go,' he said. 'The golem's getting closer. I have to get to those magi before that creature reaches the palace. I don't know if the dome will hold it back for long.'

His brother touched his bracelet. Emad felt more than heard the command. The handful of djinn who remained in Iram were to retreat to the ziggurat in the occupied half.

'What are you doing, Fiqitush?'

His brother stared at the iron dome's approach. He grimaced.

'Magic won't stop them,' he said, his voice toneless. 'Water worked. Let's see what happens when I collapse some of Iram on them.'

26

Roshan lifted Navid from the crook of her arm and placed him in her satchel. With the daevas asleep in both tents, she and Behrouz had to work fast before the incantation wore off. Surrounded by her own dome of invisibility and silence, she raised a portal into one of the two tents. Behrouz stepped through first. Roshan followed, hoping the dome collapsed only after the portal had. If that didn't happen, a passer-by might glimpse the portal's azure light.

Inside the tent, Behrouz had woven a new dome of invisibility and silence. He nodded for Roshan to collapse her portal.

The intensity of the torchlight outside made it possible for Roshan to check on how deeply the daevas slept. They'd arranged themselves head to foot along the tent's length, two to each side. The tent was only wide enough to accommodate a daeva at either end, which left the seventh daeva to lie in the middle. All of them were shackled. Roshan set to work removing the pins and heaping the manacles as far from Behrouz as the confined space allowed.

Behrouz raised a portal to Baka. On the other side of the

destination window, daevas waited to receive the remaining prisoners at a prearranged location.

Behrouz began a levitation incantation, then stopped.

'There's too much iron in here,' he said. 'I can't maintain this portal. You'll have to send them through.'

Roshan began her own incantation and then, one by one, raised each daeva—starting with the one in the middle—and directed them through the portal. The daevas in Baka positioned themselves to grab the prisoners the instant they exited the portal.

Several of the daevas stirred as they rose off the ground. Roshan didn't want to repeat the sleep incantation and risk dropping a floating daeva.

The tension along her back relaxed after the seventh daeva disappeared into the Baka. She collapsed the portal. If not for Behrouz's stoic expression, she might have grinned her relief. A second tent filled with daeva prisoners and Behrouz's eagerness to return to Iram meant they had no time to celebrate.

Roshan raised a portal to the adjacent tent. Again, Behrouz went first so he could raise a new dome of invisibility and silence.

Inside the second tent, Roshan tensed after collapsing the portal next door. She strained her ears for the sound of approaching guardsmen. After a count of five, she started to remove the daevas' manacles. They had arranged themselves similarly to those in the first tent.

'Who are you? You're not a djinni. What are you doing?'

The daeva lying in the centre of the tent had woken. Her sleep incantation must have worn off. His arms shook, making the chain between his wrists clink. Roshan leaned across to remove the manacles from his wrists. The daeva hugged himself, making it difficult for her to reach the pins.

'Don't,' he said. 'I promised the high magus we wouldn't try to escape.'

About to ask why he'd do such a thing, Roshan realised the answer.

'He used the seal on you.'

The daeva nodded, his eyes roving from Roshan to the daevas lying each side of him.

'Some of us have families. The high magus made us promise. Otherwise, he'd execute our wives and children.'

We should have located the missing daevas first, Roshan thought.

'We need to get you to Baka. Then we'll look for your families,' she said.

'Luqa, who's that you're talking to?'

The question came from the back of the tent.

'It's all right,' Luqa said. He looked at Roshan with round, pleading eyes. 'They're going. There's nothing to worry about.'

Roshan heard the clink of chains. The daeva behind Luqa sat up.

'Wait,' the daeva at the back of the tent said. 'I've seen you before.' The daeva paused, bent his head and massaged his temples.

Roshan swallowed.

'This iron makes it hard to think,' he continued. 'I saw you...in Arshak.'

An ache blossomed in Roshan's chest, and she only just stopped herself from wishing she could disappear.

The air inside the tent suddenly felt as if she were out in the noonday desert. It dried her tongue and the sweat on her forehead.

'We're here to help,' her brother said from behind her. His voice filled her ears rather than her head. She looked back and saw Navid. He must have climbed out of her satchel and shape-shifted. Beyond him, another daeva had woken. This one reached with both manacled hands for Behrouz's ankle.

'Behrouz,' she said, pointing.

Behrouz sidestepped the grasping hands, only to have the

daeva lying on the opposite side of the tent reach for him and yell. The touch of iron against his foot buckled Behrouz's knees. He fell forward, knocking Navid against the tent's side. Behrouz landed on the daeva called Luqa and then struggled to rise.

Blades punctured the tent's canvas and slashed downward.

Navid cried out as the tip of a blade cut into his side.

Guardsmen pushed through the tears.

All the muscles in Roshan's body stiffened until she no longer moved. Roshan remembered Daniyel's body lying in the alleyway, his neck broken. The image made it hard to think, to know what to do to help her brother and Behrouz.

With a loud *pop* the tent—canvas, poles and guy ropes—flew up and into the night.

Yesfir stood next to the tent they'd emptied earlier. For a moment, no one moved. Roshan's muscles uncoiled, but the ache in her chest remained. A guardsman stepped towards Yesfir. Roshan recognised the first words of the djinni's incantation and ducked.

The force behind the pulse of hot air threw Roshan onto her side and knocked the wind from her. Her ears rang as she righted herself. Navid appeared above her, his face resembling a skull. His skeletal hands held hers. She noticed prominent ribs, the ligaments of his elbows and kneecaps that looked too large for his legs. He must have recognised her concern.

'I was injured, so I transformed. I've done it three times without drinking water.' His words were just audible about the ringing in her ears. 'Don't worry.' He pointed with his chin at Behrouz. 'We should help him.'

Purple illuminated the sand. Ahead of them stood Yesfir's portal, its destination window pointed at Baka.

A guardsman and a daeva lay on top of Behrouz. Dazed, the guardsman rolled off with a tug. Roshan hesitated. The daeva was unconscious.

'Help me,' Navid said. 'I can't lift him off on my own.'

She gripped the daeva by the ankles and waited for Navid to lift him by the shoulders. Roshan felt happy at the daevas' unconsciousness. Why would Yesfir rendering a daeva unconscious make her happy?

Behrouz groaned but didn't get up.

'Yesfir's here,' Navid said.

At the mention of her name, Behrouz tried to sit up. Navid and Roshan took a shoulder each and pushed.

'What's she doing here?' he said. 'It's not safe.'

'She's rescuing us, stupid,' Navid said.

Roshan glared at her brother.

'It's the iron,' she whispered. 'It's affecting him.'

They had to steer Behrouz until he recognised the portal. With each step, he seemed more certain, more clear-headed.

At the portal, he said, 'You two go first. I'll wait for Yesfir.'

Seeing her brother so emaciated and in need of water, she said, 'You go. Don't wait around. Get yourself some water—lots.'

Navid smiled. An instant before it collapsed, he stepped into the portal.

Roshan cried out and swung round.

Yesfir had her back to them. The high magus stood to one side of her, his hand outstretched. The seal on his middle finger glinted in the torchlight.

Roshan raised an open hand, ready to squeeze Sassan's throat, and then hesitated. What if she ended up strangling Yesfir, too?

'Yesfir!' Behrouz yelled. He passed Roshan, obscuring her view of the high magus as he dashed towards his wife.

Roshan caught movement from the corner of her eye. More guardsmen had arrived, and three of the conscious daevas crawled through the sand towards the high magus.

Sassan looked away from Yesfir and shifted his attention onto her and Behrouz. Behrouz's back stiffened and he dug his heels into the sand as he fought the seal's influence.

Roshan experienced an emptiness creep into her. It turned

her insides into stone and banished her will to where it retreated during sleep.

'No,' she said, resisting the compulsion.

The emptiness shrank away. She drew in a deep breath.

Behrouz took a step towards the high magus.

I don't want us to be here.

She closed her eyes to the blinding orange light, then opened them.

She and Behrouz, but not Yesfir, stood in front of Iram's palace. To her left, and in front of her, buildings collapsed. Above the din, Roshan heard Behrouz cry out his wife's name.

27

E mad raised his first portal in eighteen years. He glanced to his side. The orange flames around Fiqitush's irises blazed the instant his brother summoned Core power and began his incantation. Emad imagined how his brother must look to the soldiers approaching the palace: a powerful and unpredictable djinni.

Be careful, he thought.

He'd only been back in Iram for three days, and Emad wasn't sure how he'd cope if anything happened to his brother.

Fiqitush glanced across at him.

'What are you waiting for? Go.'

I'm getting soft, Emad thought, and stepped into the portal.

Moonlight was all that lit the opposite end of the city. Emad had arrived on a street leading to a bridge over the canal. A shattered pot lay in front of him, the soil and the plant it contained dry and flaky. Water lapped against the canal bank, and behind him the windows of the surrounding homes were shuttered or curtained by darkness. To his left, and farther behind the houses, loomed the ziggurat. He knew the handful of remaining djinn watched from behind domes of invisibility and silence.

Once he'd raised a dome, Emad headed for and crossed the bridge onto the main road. A distant rumble came from the palace. A loud crash echoed off the cavern's walls.

Before him, the unoccupied half of the city stretched into the distance. Emad felt foolish. With so many empty buildings, it would take him forever to find the magi—assuming they hadn't hidden themselves under a dome. His stomach twisted. If he didn't find the magi soon, there'd be no point finding them at all.

Emad stepped onto the towpath. The debris of the city's former occupants filled the dry waterway next to it. He jogged towards the palace, scanning the streets on his right, hoping to find some clue to the magi's whereabouts.

Two hundred steps later, Emad cursed himself for his lack of fitness. Before he'd settled in Derbicca with Aeshma, he could climb up and down *Apkallu*'s mainmast without breaking a sweat. Emad stopped, rested his hands on his knees and fought for breath.

You're as much use as a cross-eyed lookout, he told himself.

Emad straightened. A three-storey building in the street opposite gave him an idea. He collapsed the dome hiding him, raised a portal and stepped onto the building's roof. A quick search of the street below and those two up from where he stood revealed nothing.

It seemed a good idea.

His next portal deposited him on the roof of a building, a courtyard at its centre. Again, from this vantage point, he saw nothing in the street below and the one opposite. He trod around the fallen bricks and dried mortar to reach the facing wall.

A loud *clang* came from behind him.

The palace, he thought. *I'm too late.*

He summoned Core power but didn't recite the incantation for a destination window to the palace. Down below, in the street opposite, a green light that matched the symbol on the golem's chest pulsed from a window.

Emad's portal deposited him two doors down from the glow. With a dome of invisibility and silence enveloping him, he strode to the terraced shop. He pressed his back against the wall next to the window and peeked in.

Two magi stood over a rock and recited incantations. The rock, cut from the cavern's wall, had a symbol carved onto its surface. If he could end the magi's incantation, destroy the symbol or both, he'd stop the golem.

Multiple *clangs* echoed around the cavern.

From the metallic ring, Emad guessed the golem had clashed with something other than Fiqitush's protective dome. He still had time to act.

Emad collapsed his dome and then, using his aura, reached into the room the magi occupied. Instead of the magi's auras, he experienced an unyielding resistance. He retreated from the room. They'd erected a dome of protection around themselves.

No surprise there.

He stepped back from the building and away from the window. He chewed his lower lip. Even if he brought down the roof, the dome of protection would protect the magi.

Emad bumped the heel of his hand against his forehead.

Idiot.

It didn't matter if the magi survived. A building collapsing around them would have to, at least, distract them and interrupt the incantations. Emad summoned a portal onto the roof of the building opposite the magi.

Below, the intensity of the green light rose and fell as if in time with a heartbeat.

Emad's incantation shook the building so hard, the roof fell in first, followed by two walls. He waited for the rock and masonry to settle and then squinted to see if any light escaped from among gaps in the debris. From behind him came the sound of metal striking rock. In front of him, a *creak* followed by a loud *screech* dampened the background hammering.

The flat roof, having splintered into three pieces, sank deeper into the ruined building. The shattered sections then rose, one of which slid onto the street. A wall, its top third torn away when the roof had collapsed, tottered and then fell backwards and onto the neighbouring shop.

Emad groaned and rubbed his face. The magi's dome of protection expanded in all directions, clearing away the fallen masonry and releasing more green light into the unconfined space.

You would have done more damage if you'd sneezed on them.

The magi within the dome continued their recitations, although their heads turned left, right, up and down to locate the source of the earthquake.

Emad crouched. His jaw ached from gritting his teeth. What was he going to do now? He glanced over at the ziggurat in Iram's occupied half.

Go over there and get some help. We could squash that dome and the buggers inside.

Emad stood, not caring if the magi saw him. A flash of orange came from behind him. Emad turned to see a portal in front of the palace, its rim bright orange. He tried to recall whose portal produced such a vibrant colour.

The *clangs* became frenzied. In the time it took to decide between heading over to the palace instead of the ziggurat, both the hammering and the incantations stopped. The light from the portal winked out. Emad squinted so hard, his forehead burned. He turned. In the shop across from him, the symbol in the rock had gone out. Emad dropped into a squat.

Below, the magi stumbled over the building's wreckage. Together, they ran down the street and then turned left.

Where are you two off to?

147

He continued to watch as the pair made their way onto the main road and ran towards the path up and out of Iram.

An incantation later, Emad held a scimitar. He'd head them off and then stop them.

'Wait,' he muttered to himself. He shook the scimitar, and it evaporated. 'They might be more use alive. See what they do first.' He touched his bracelet and whispered, 'Fiqitush.'

Emad sighed. His brother was well.

He raised a portal and arrived beneath an arch overlooking Iram. In the distance and on his right, Fiqitush had reduced the buildings in a small section of the unoccupied half of Iram to rubble. His brother had also collapsed the dome of protection encasing the palace.

Good, he thought.

Emad raised a dome of invisibility and silence and then waited for the two magi to reach the tunnel and the city's exit.

28

Roshan flinched at Behrouz's black look.

'Why did you do that? Yesfir needed our help.'

The ground shook and dust filled the air as a building to her left collapsed. Behrouz seemed oblivious to the destruction and to how the seal had controlled him.

The seal.

Its power had driven out her wants and needs so it could influence the rest of her.

'The seal,' she said to Behrouz. 'It had Yesfir, and it almost took you.'

Her words made her sick. Yesfir had rescued them, and they'd left her behind in Arshak. *She'd* left Yesfir in Arshak.

Behrouz pulled off his bracelet and let it drop to the floor.

In front of her, the king emerged from a dust cloud.

'I have to conserve my auric energy to save Yesfir,' Behrouz said. 'I'm less of a djinn without my bracelet, and I'll be able to resist the seal. Send me back to Arshak.'

Roshan picked up the bracelet. The muscles surrounding her lower back twinged with pain and soreness. She remembered how Yesfir had hurled everyone to the ground with an incantation. Given the circumstances, she'd had little choice. Rather than do nothing, Yesfir had risked the safety of others to protect those dear to her.

Right now, she had to risk Yesfir's safety to protect Behrouz.

'Yesfir saved us, Behrouz,' she said. 'If you go back, there's no guarantee you'll be able to resist the seal. I also felt it working on me. That's why we're here. You returning to Arshak on your own isn't the way to get her back.' She held up the bracelet.

'Behrouz, Roshan, what are you doing here? You need to leave.'

The king strode towards them. The dust behind him had settled, revealing heaps of rock, brick and rubble.

'Emad wasn't able to stop the magi,' he said. 'You have to leave —*now.*'

Roshan looked past the king and saw his cause for concern.

She had only heard about them and had never seen one. The shattered rock and brick that composed its thickset limbs made its movements ponderous. The golem, however, moved with slow, deliberate, unstoppable malice.

She looked at her hand and found she no longer had the bracelet. Behrouz held it for a moment, his eyes glazed. His head dropped forward, and his face crumpled as if something inside of him had broken. He slipped the bracelet back onto his wrist, raised his head and strode past the king. A hammer materialised in his hand. The diameter of its brass head was as wide as a man's chest.

King Fiqitush joined her. Together, they watched Behrouz lope towards the golem.

'I don't think he'll be able to stop it on his own,' the king said.

It was twice Behrouz's height and made of rock; Roshan agreed.

Behrouz swung the hammer as if he always held one. It struck the centre of the glowing symbol. Stone shards erupted from the golem's chest, and the force of the blow sent it skidding back a step. The golem raised a cumbersome hand, ready to strike. Behrouz ignored it and swung at the symbol again. More splinters of rock erupted from the golem's chest.

'Look,' the king said, then pointed.

The shards of fallen rock around the golem's feet rolled towards it. When they touched a foot, they disappeared, as if sucked back into the golem, reabsorbed.

Behrouz ducked the golem's backhand swipe, leaned back and swung again at the symbol. The blow rooted the golem to the spot—momentarily. It pressed forward, forcing Behrouz backwards.

Behrouz can only slow it down, she thought. *There's no way he'll stop it.*

Roshan stepped forward and raised a portal behind the golem. The destination window opened onto a mountain range. Starlight turned its three snow-capped peaks silver.

Behrouz sidestepped and swung the hammer at the golem's right side. He darted behind its back and reappeared in front of it. He hammered at its left side.

The power behind his strikes only damaged the golem's surface. They lacked sufficient force to drive it backwards and into the portal.

Roshan closed her eyes, touched her bracelet and imagined Domain energy passing from her into Behrouz.

Be stronger, she thought.

She opened her eyes. Behrouz staggered and dropped onto a knee.

What have I done?

The golem raised both hands, its palms open, ready to squash Behrouz between them. Roshan held her breath. She'd decided to turn the golem to dust and blow it through the portal when, still clutching the hammer, Behrouz rolled. Back on his feet, he positioned himself just in front and to the side of the golem's right. The hammer smashed through the golem's side.

Roshan saw her chance and rushed forward. She called out an incantation and almost tripped over bricks rolling back to rejoin the golem. With the last word of the incantation uttered, she directed the current of air with a hand and blew the bricks past the golem and into the portal.

Meanwhile, Behrouz had swivelled around to the golem's left flank and knocked a chunk from it.

'Its legs,' the king called.

The king hurried past her and repeated the same incantation. She blew the remnants of the golem's side into the portal. Behrouz got to work on its leg. He swung the hammer as if wielding an axe. Rock scattered everywhere, and the golem fell forward. Behrouz shattered its hand in the same instant it touched the ground.

Roshan and the king had to keep moving to find positions from which they could blow pieces of the golem, and not Behrouz, into the portal. The sound of rock scraping against itself and splitting hurt her ears.

A new hand and a new calf and then a foot burst from the golem's stumps. The rocks' and bricks' redistribution, however, caused it to contract in size.

Undeterred, Behrouz continued to hammer and swipe at the golem, alternating his attacks from one leg to the other. Roshan and the king moved in arcs, sweeping away the broken pieces of the creature. Each time their paths crossed, she noticed the same expression on Behrouz's face.

His brow notched, and his normally gentle eyes conveyed a relentless fury Roshan had never seen in the two years she'd known him. She understood, not because she could empathise but because she'd touched her bracelet and connected with him.

Behrouz was furious with himself for being weak and unable to resist the seal. Their having to leave Yesfir behind had snapped something inside of him. He'd be out of balance and unsure of himself until Yesfir was safe and back at his side.

As the golem shrank, their pace quickened, Behrouz knocking away at it—piece by piece—and Roshan and the king blowing the debris into the portal. It wasn't long before Behrouz and the golem were the same size. Behrouz dropped the hammer —turning to smoke before it hit the ground—ducked under the golem's arm and came up behind it. The golem turned too late. Behrouz grabbed it by the shoulder and between the legs and hoisted it above his head. With baleful eyes, he turned and flung the golem, its arms flailing, into the portal.

Roshan blew what remained of the golem into the portal and then collapsed it. Her bracelet pulsed with Fiqitush's order for the djinn to return.

Portals appeared and djinn approached the king, who issued orders.

Roshan stood beside the kneeling Behrouz and put a hand on his shoulder.

'You were right,' he said, looking abashed. 'I'd have succumbed to the seal.'

'I know,' she said. 'It's your bracelet—I experienced your thoughts.'

His brow furrowed.

'Then you know I have to save her.'

Roshan nodded. She looked over at the king who continued directing the djinn.

'But first we have to tell him. He needs to know. Then we'll decide how to save her.'

29

Emad sat on a rock. Dawn's chilly air penetrated his dome of invisibility and silence and made him shiver. He guessed the two magi sitting on the sand ten paces ahead of him, and under their own dome, were cold too. As the light brightened, Emad saw the outline of a crescent-shaped outcrop. It reminded him of a viper sunning itself.

Last night, he'd followed the magi up the passageway leading to Iram's hidden exit and, once they'd raised a dome, traced their footsteps in the wind-smoothed sand. The two men hadn't gone far—around the corner from the cave's entrance and behind it— before they'd stopped. He half-expected a portal to appear. Indentations appeared in the sand where they'd sat down.

Six hours later, none of the soldiers from below had appeared, and no one had collected the magi.

Emad touched his bracelet to check on Fiqitush. He sensed the determination keeping his brother's exhaustion at bay. Emad perceived something else. It felt like simultaneous relief and sadness.

His fingertips hovered over the silver band for a second touch. Emad shook his head. Although he wanted to, he couldn't bring himself to reach out to either Roshan or Navid. He didn't want to make them uncomfortable or question why he'd done such a thing.

So much had happened in the four days following his rescue from Derbicca. Just two days earlier, his brother had informed him of his paternity. Emad still reeled from that news. It hadn't taken long to accept Fiqitush's reason for keeping the twins a secret from him. He'd only known their mother, Shafira, for less than a week. She'd gotten to know him well enough in that short time to know he'd make a lousy father. He hadn't wanted the responsibility that came with his title. So, why would he want to be tied down by children?

After so long, how do I make it up to them? he wondered.

Emad pondered the question. No immediate answer came. Roshan and Navid had done well enough without him. How would it help, their knowing he was their father?

Soldiers, five, carrying swords and shields, appeared out of mid-air. Emad's chilled bones made it hard to stand up.

The two magi flickered and then solidified. They walked towards the men.

Emad took a step and stopped.

The soldiers carried iron shields. Ten more paces and they'd leave him incapacitated. Then, seeing the high magus emerge behind the soldiers, Emad growled his frustration.

Emad cast his eye about for something real, physical and non-magical to hurl at or drop on the high magus. Thanks to their shields, anything magical, like the wind his brother had whipped up and flung at the soldiers down in Iram, would fizzle out. A flash of green drew his attention back to the group.

Emad saw a daeva merge the destination and boarding windows. Without touching his bracelet and alerting him, Emad couldn't tell how much the daeva had struggled before falling under the seal's influence.

All he could do was stand and watch while the two magi,

their heads bowed, entered the portal. Through a gap in the soldiers' cordon, Emad spied how the high magus's eyelids drooped and his eyes hardly blinked. Emad recognised the stupor poppy juice produced. He's seen it on the faces of lounging noblemen during his visits to Kemet. If the high magus was using the stuff, it might make him vulnerable.

It will also make him unpredictable.

The thought made Emad shiver. When he'd first encountered the high magus in Derbicca, Emad saw nothing to suggest that Sassan, like his other magi, used poppy juice. What had happened? Why was he using it now?

Stiff and slow, the high magus turned and disappeared into the portal. One by one, the soldiers did the same. Their shields' repulsive force decreased, making it easier for Emad to approach the portal.

Without realising he'd recited the incantation, Emad held a scimitar. The speed of his decision stunned him.

The high magus knew Iram's location. Thanks to the seal, he had the means of returning again and again. But what of Baka? After the trouble caused by a dozen soldiers and a golem, what kind of chaos could he unleash on hundreds of daevas living in tents?

Emad tightened his grip on the scimitar's hilt. From the daeva's behaviour, it looked as though the seal continued to exert its influence all the way from Arshak. If he could hand the sword to another, let them perform the deed, he wouldn't. He was doing this for all those in Iram and everyone just waking up in Baka. Emad also thought of Navid and Roshan. He'd do this as much for them as the djinn and daevas.

The daeva probably had a family, one that might already be in Baka, worrying about him. It wasn't his fault he was here, helping the high magus. But his sacrifice would set back the high magus's plans and buy the djinn and daevas more time.

He thought about collapsing his dome of invisibility and

silence but decided it would be a kindness if the daeva didn't know what was about to happen to him.

The last soldier stepped through the portal. Emad raised the scimitar and closed the three paces between him and the daeva.

'Sorry, brother,' Emad said, and then cut off the daeva's head.

30

Dwarfed by the palace's double doorway, Roshan watched the djinn departing through the king's mauve portal. They had returned from Baka for their belongings, which they carried as bundles tucked under their arms. Some helped carry trunks filled with tablets and papyri taken from Iram's library. The children herded the goats that had descended the cavern's walls soon after dawn—they, like the eagles, knew the djinn were leaving.

Except for the goats' bleats and the odd cry of surprise as an eagle swooped into the portal, the line of djinn was silent. Roshan couldn't tell if it was tiredness, resignation at leaving their home sooner than later, or both that stooped their shoulders and dulled their eyes.

Navid appeared at her side. He carried a bag under his arm.

'Is that everything?' she said.

Rested, he'd returned from Baka just before dawn.

Navid patted the bag, then nodded.

'Not much to show for two years,' he said.

Navid was joking. Their possessions didn't reflect how events over the past eight days had changed them and their situation.

Her brother scanned the line of djinn. They left through a single portal so Shephatiah could log what they carried with them into Baka.

'Where's Behrouz?'

Roshan closed her eyes and held her breath for a count of five.

'He left for Baka just after dawn. He wanted to tell Zana what's happened to Yesfir before the news spread.' She bowed her head.

'Hey,' Navid said, and gave her a one-armed hug, 'it's not your fault.'

She shook her head.

'It's not that. The king's prohibited anyone from launching a rescue until Iram is evacuated.'

Navid looked to be considering the reasoning behind such a command.

'Now that the high magus has the seal, trying to rescue Yesfir won't be as straightforward as Derbicca was—and that wasn't straightforward.'

Navid was right, but that wasn't why Roshan found it difficult to accept the command.

'Yesfir's his daughter,' she said. 'It can't have been easy to decide such a thing. I know he wants to avoid other djinn being captured, but still, she's his daughter.'

Navid pointed at Emad. The prince stood next to the king with his hands behind his back. Emad's brow furrowed whenever he looked at his brother.

'Looks like he doesn't agree with the decision either.'

Roshan slipped from under Navid's arm and strolled towards the queue.

'Earlier this morning, when I went to the king's chambers—I wanted to apologise for what had happened to Yesfir. I heard him arguing with the prince. I didn't want to eavesdrop, so I knocked on the door. The argument was about the king and not Yesfir.'

They joined the queue of djinn, which had shortened since Navid's arrival with their belongings. Roshan surveyed the city. Apart from the obvious destruction close to the palace, Iram looked no different to when she'd first seen it. Now, even with the sun's rays lighting rooftops and clearing the streets of shadows, the city felt empty and already forgotten. She tried to imagine how Iram might have been one or two centuries before, the markets above the docks busy, boats leaving and entering through portals and the flurry of life echoing off the cavern's walls.

Could the king turn Baka into a new Iram? she wondered. *Now the high magus possesses the seal, is it right to even think such a thing? How hopeful are the djinn about starting new lives under such conditions?*

'I doubt we'll see this place again,' Navid said.

She nodded. Her brother was right.

But this couldn't have been how the king imagined the djinn would leave Iram, their home for three centuries. The djinn and daevas settling into Baka, making it their new home, would have to wait until, somehow, they separated the seal from the high magus and found a way to end his persecution of the daevas.

Just a few steps from the portal, Roshan resolved to protect them all. Her dithering, her thinking too much about the consequences of using sabaoth magic, caused Yesfir's capture. Once all the djinn were in Baka, she'd help Behrouz rescue Yesfir. Then, if she had to, she'd weave sabaoth magic and deal with the consequences later.

END OF BOOK 2

———

THE BAKA DJINN Chronicles continue with *City of Daevas.*

High Magus Sassan and his army appear outside a sand-filled and crumbling Baka. If she's going to help the djinn and daevas ready the city for war, Roshan must put aside her desire to take the fight to the high magus. Doing so, however, will leave her weak and vulnerable.

Meanwhile, worried about Yesfir, Behrouz and Zana are desperate to rescue her. When ordered to remain in Baka, Zana goes in search of the Cross Scar manticores for help.

As guardsmen and golems being their attack on Baka, Roshan must make an impossible choice, one that will either save the djinn and daevas or doom Baka and its inhabitants to endless slavery.

A NOTE FROM THE AUTHOR

Thank you for reading this book. This book is part of the first trilogy in the Baka Chronicles. Reader reviews will help me determine whether to keep the series going. Whether it's brief or detailed, your feedback will make a huge difference.

ABOUT THE AUTHOR

J F Mehentee is a British-born Asian with Persian ancestry. A lifelong reader of fantasy and science fiction, he's always looking for ways to combine his interest in Asian and Middle Eastern mythology with storytelling.

After spending three years in Phnom Penh, Cambodia, he now lives in Colombo, Sri Lanka, where he writes full-time—all the while dreaming of one day playing jazz flute like Ron Burgundy.

To learn more, visit www.jfmehentee.com.

ACKNOWLEDGMENTS

Producing the Baka Chronicles has been a team effort. I couldn't have created this series without help from the following professionals:

Structural editor: James Christy,
Copy editor: Richard Shealy,
Cover designer: Deranged Doctor Design.

Finally, huge THANK YOUs to Ginny for her love and encouragement and to my brother, V, who's read just about everything I've ever written—first drafts included!

Published by P in C Publishing

ISBN: 978-1-912402-21-2